More praise for *Dancing at the Harvest Moon*

"Perfectly balanced fiction, artful, and agreeably written . . . Compact and as gracefully flowing as scarlet leaves on a Canadian lake in autumn, *Dancing at the Harvest Moon* is a love story, a mature romance."

—*Jackson Clarion-Ledger*

"Entertaining . . . The novel tells the story of a May-December romance, only with a new twist. . . . It also carries the upbeat message that sometimes life offers us a second chance."

—*Fitchburg Sentinel & Enterprise* (MA)

"A winner . . . McKinnon tells a tender, bittersweet tale. . . . *Dancing at the Harvest Moon* is a refreshing novel, intelligently written."

—*Sunday World Herald*

"A tender tale about a woman's second chance at first love."

—*Courier-Journal* (Louisville, KY)

"Entrancing."

—*BookPage*

By K. C. McKinnon (who is also Cathie Pelletier):

DANCING AT THE HARVEST MOON*
CANDLES ON BAY STREET

By Cathie Pelletier:

THE FUNERAL MAKERS
ONCE UPON A TIME ON THE BANKS
THE WEIGHT OF WINTER
THE BUBBLE REPUTATION
A MARRIAGE MADE AT WOODSTOCK
BEAMING SONNY HOME

THE CHRISTMAS NOTE (with Skeeter Davis)
A COUNTRY MUSIC CHRISTMAS (Editor)

Poems
WIDOWS WALK

**Published by Fawcett Books*

DANCING AT THE HARVEST MOON

K.C. McKinnon

FAWCETT BOOKS • NEW YORK

A Fawcett Crest Book
Published by The Ballantine Publishing Group

www.randomhouse.com/BB/

Library of Congress Catalog Card Number: 98-96985

ISBN 0-449-00527-5

This edition published by arrangement with Doubleday, a division of Random House, Inc.

Manufactured in the United States of America

First Ballantine Books Edition: April 1999

10 9 8 7 6 5 4 3 2 1

ACKNOWLEDGMENTS

For **Tom Viorikic**, who convinced me to "write a different kind of book," and who also loves those blue herons, and those blue Canadian lakes.

For **Carl E. Hileman**, my friend for two decades, who did the illustrations. If Robert Flaubert ever took human form, it would be as Carl, who lives with nature while he paints and writes songs in a house he built for himself, in Southern Illinois.

For the Harvest Moon Gang, in honor of our ritual gathering on the shores of Lake Katchewanooka, that little Canadian lake where I first got the idea for this book: **Tom Viorikic, Snezana & Dusko Knezevic, Lizzie & Danny Perovic, Peter & Julie Pellegris; Eliza Clark** (including **Michael & Arden**), **Sue, Rick & Jennifer Browning** (whose cottages there offer a perfect haven); and for the loons, squirrels, chipmunks, beavers, and raccoons. And, of course, those great blue herons, who are probably still fishing off the dock in the early morning mist.

For the Doubleday Gang: **Arlene Friedman, Pat Mulcahy, Denell Downum, Kathy Hale, Amy King, Lawrence Krauser, Carol Lazare, Robin Swados, and Paula Breen**, for all the hard work.

For **Mother and Father**, as always. And to the memory of my Canadian ancestors, both paternal and maternal.

And in memory of **Augusta McKinnon**.

Thank you, **Neil Young**, for such a beautiful song as "Harvest Moon."

DANCING AT THE HARVEST MOON

The Moon, 1967

A LACE HANDKERCHIEF

> It had become a glimmering girl
> with apple blossom in her hair,
> who called me by my name and ran,
> and faded through the brightening air.
> —William Butler Yeats

It isn't always just before you die that your whole life flashes before your eyes. That's a physical kind of dying, but it's not the only kind. For some people, there comes a day when every dream they ever piled up over the years, every good intention rises up in rebellion against the life they've been living. It can happen on the subway, behind the wheel of a car, while standing on a bridge looking down at the water. It can occur at the Laundromat, a bingo parlor, at McDonald's. It can happen early in the morning, while you're sitting over a bowl of oatmeal. Maybe it's the smell that reminds you of an earlier day when you still dared to dream. Or it might be an old song that brings back to you your younger self, a daring self, a butterfly waiting. However it happens, wherever it happens, whenever it happens, one thing is certain: You die and then you're reborn. This is what happened to Maggie Ann McIntyre while rifling through a trunk of old souvenirs in search of a term paper she'd written twenty-five years earlier, a paper she had titled "W. B. Yeats: Symbolism, Mythology and the Occult." She had promised Jennifer Fulbright, who was also doing a paper on Yeats, that she would look for it among the boxes in her attic. After all, Jennifer was her best student. Sometimes in class, when Maggie looked up quickly from her paperwork and saw Jennifer's head tilted, chin in hand, the sun lighting up the auburn sparks in her hair, she felt as if she were looking at her younger self, the university student, twenty-one years old and ready to begin studies for a master's degree. A glimmering girl. But it wasn't she. It was Jennifer Fulbright, lounging in modern sunlight, an intelligent young girl who had also fallen in love with the lyrical world of Yeats and now wanted to read what her professor had had to say about the poet. So Maggie had left her father and his wife, Vivian, having coffee in the tiny parlor, their suitcases sitting like patient dogs by the front door, and she had gone up into the attic to find the boxes marked COLLEGE PAPERS. Lifting the lid, she'd expected to probe through yellowing pages of words written from 1965 to 1969, her years spent at Boston University. Before graduate school. Before theses and dissertations and marriage and two children. And it was there, in the heat of the attic, with summer rising up outside the brown Victorian house that had been home for so many years on Beauchemin Street in Kansas City, Missouri, that Maggie had what she might have told her students was a regular James Joyce *epiphany*, "a sudden revelation of the essential nature of a thing, person or situation." She didn't find the paper on Yeats. Instead, as she fingered through old exams, her hand touched upon something soft and fragile hiding at the bottom of a box: It was a frayed handkerchief, a soft wishlike thing with a white lace border, given to her by the first boy she had ever loved, had ever made love with, a boy whose tender heart she had broken. And while she could never forget him as the years came and went, she never let him be anything more than a quiet ghost, following her through the movie of her life, a ghost she still loved in that young and innocent way, but a ghost nonetheless.

It was hardly the day for it, what with her students waiting to take their final exam in World Lit. It was hardly the place for it, a stifling attic, her father and Vivian downstairs waiting to be driven to the airport. But that's when it happened. She had a genuine epiphany: She would go back to the Harvest Moon, the dance hall where she'd worked all those summers ago. She would go to Canada and search for her younger self, the girl who reminded her of Jennifer, the girl with a long lovely future ahead of her. She would look for that ghost of a boy, her first love, Robert Flaubert, sweet Robbie, a boy she had believed she might one day marry until graduate school carried her away from him, until time carried her down its river into a new life where he couldn't follow. She would go to that lovely lake in Canada, where the Harvest Moon hugged the shores, where loons cried out in the long swatches of the evening. She would go back to where she had made her first great mistake—breaking Rob Flaubert's heart—and maybe then she'd know what the next move in her life could be, *should* be. For the truth was, this wasn't life she had been living. This was mere existence.

With dust particles from the box of old papers rising up in a stream of sunlight, Maggie breathed deeply. She listened to the flutter of birds entering the eaves outside. For the first time in almost a year she felt safe again. She felt in control. The house seemed to be wrapped around her like good solid arms, protecting her. And why shouldn't it? After all, this was where Maggie had moved with a young husband she met in 1969 at graduate school, Joe McIntyre, and then married in 1970. This was the house that had protected them from wind and rain and snow for over twenty years. This was the house they had filled with two decades of plants, and a half-dozen beloved pets, all gone back to their maker. This was the brown Victorian, with the hydrangeas growing up on each side of the front steps and rose of Sharon in the backyard, a house that saw two babies come in through its doors, babies it kept safe from winter storms and rain-filled winds and summer sun, until they grew old enough, and strong enough, to walk out through its doors again for good, only to return on holidays and the occasional vacation. And it was a house that saw her struggle as a part-time student and mom, a house that saw her through night classes, and then full-time day classes after the girls started school themselves, until Maggie had received a doctorate in Comparative Literature. This was the house that sheltered the man she had married all those evenings when he came home from his law firm, tired and sweaty, his head swimming with precedents and briefs and the pretty young paralegal with the trim thighs who finally convinced him that he could be young again in her arms, in her bed, in her life. Joe's own *glimmering girl*. Up until that point in time, until just nine months ago, the sturdy brown Victorian had been a house that sheltered Maggie, too, looming up before her eyes each afternoon as she turned the corner of Drake and Beauchemin, tired from a day of Eliot and Pound and Hardy and Tolstoy, and university students who mostly didn't care about words of the heart and mind. Until the young paralegal changed all that. Until Joe asked Maggie if he could talk to her, in the lovely little parlor with the fireplace, and the glass case with her prized first editions of Faulkner and Millay and Wilde. She knew then, by the tension in his face, the tautness in the muscles of his handsome face, a face she had always expected to see until the day one of them died and left the other behind, that something was terribly wrong. Her mind had raced with possibilities, the most horrible kind of possibilities, unspeakable to any parent: *One of the children has died! There has been an accident and Diana or Lucy is dead.* Diana, tall and slim, named for Maggie's mother. Lucinda, the dark, brooding one who took after Joe, who carried his mother's name. *Something has happened to Diana or Lucy!* But it hadn't. The girls were safe in their own cities, in the tiny apartments they shared with other roommates, Diana's the boy she had brought home that past Christmas to meet the family. A commercial artist, he worked for the same ad agency as she, in Chicago. And Lucy, well, Lucy would be harder for some young man to snag, Lucy who was just entering graduate school at Boston University, a career as a microbiologist ahead. Her roommates were other studious young women who shared her interests of backpacking and mountain climbing. No, the girls were, thankfully, safe. Maggie, instead, had been the one in peril.

And so Maggie had sat before the fire that early October afternoon in the tiny parlor, while the maples on Beauchemin Street raged with their own scarlet fire, and she had listened as Joe unraveled the tapestry of their lives together. Her first thought had been of the young woman, Bridgette something. Maggie had only met her once, when she'd stopped to pick up Joe one day at his office. They were meeting Diana at the airport and then going out to dinner. Now, when she thought back to it, the affair must have been going on even then, for Bridgette had turned scarlet at the sight of her, as scarlet as the rock maples in all the front yards on Beauchemin Street. At the time, Maggie thought that it was her sudden appearance that had done it. Bridgette had been on the phone when she walked in, and it was obvious by her laughter, by the way she was twirling her hair with one long, slender finger, that it wasn't a business call. And so Maggie had assumed that the blushing was for being caught in the act by the boss's wife. How little she knew, looking back on that afternoon. Perhaps all logic had been replaced by the fact that within an hour Diana would be home, witty, cheerful Diana, and the brown Victorian wouldn't be as lonely as it had become with the girls gone, with Joe working longer hours than ever. Maggie remembered thinking that the blush had made Bridgette even more beautiful, the blush of youth, of promise. Then Joe told her, *I'm in love with someone else, Maggie. I'm so very, very sorry. But I want a chance to start over. I want a chance to lead another life*. She had finally taken her eyes off the glass case holding Wilde and Faulkner and Millay, and she had asked, "Who?" When he answered, "Bridgette," her first thought was of the blush that afternoon that had spread like a sunrise across Bridgette's lovely face. *Red sky at morning, sailors take warning.* She could say nothing for a minute—was it a minute or hours, maybe days?—sitting there before the fire. With the fireplace snapping from a hardwood blaze, with the autumn leaves burning up Beauchemin Street, it was no longer Bridgette who mattered. She looked up at Joe then, her husband who had been the young law student when they met, at the football game Boston won against the University of Connecticut in the fall of 1969. She kept her eyes on Joe as he hovered by the mantelpiece, looking sheepish, almost. "I wonder if you know what you've done," she had finally said to him. This wasn't about Bridgette, after all. This wasn't about a young impressionable woman just a few years older than Lucinda. This was about a middle-aged man, a man turning fifty, as Maggie herself would be doing in just four years. And it was about another man Maggie knew, a younger man. It was about the law student who wanted a family so urgently that Maggie had dropped out of school to have the babies. Maggie looked at Joe closely now, waited until he was forced to stare into her eyes. "I wonder if you can even realize," she'd said again. And then she had poured a glass of sherry, and put another chunk of wood on the fire, and sat quietly in the little parlor until Joe packed the things he couldn't do without. She felt his hand on her shoulder—as if this would ease her pain!—before he slipped silently out the front door. She heard his car backing out of the drive, backing out of his promise, backing out of her life. Then he was gone. A late autumn storm had risen up outside, bringing with it cracking thunder and soft quick flashes of lightning. Maggie had waited there alone, in the brown Victorian house that had given its life to her family's comfort. She had sipped another glass of sherry and then, as the fire died down and the only sounds in the house came from the excited fluttering of sparrows in a tree by the parlor window, she remembered something by John Keats, a poem she dearly loved. " 'And they are gone: aye, ages long ago,' " she had said, as the evening chill crept slowly up her arms. " 'These lovers fled away into the storm.' "

And so it was that almost a year later she had come to the attic to have her Great Epiphany. It had been a year of nights when all she did was lie awake in her bed and watch the moon move across the path of her bedroom window. A year of listening to the wind rustling its way up and down Beauchemin Street. A year of endless days through which she stood before a class of fresh young faces, discussing Dickens and Hardy, Emerson and Thoreau. A year that saw Halloween come and go, with trick-or-treaters who pounded on her door until they tired of it and went away. On Thanksgiving she watched Monty Python tapes and ate spaghetti and lied to everyone who phoned up with concern. "I'm having dinner with Anita," she told the girls. "The girls are coming for Thanksgiving," she told Anita. When her birthday arrived in early December and her friend Anita Wodehouse prodded her into going out for dinner at the new Thai restaurant on Danner Boulevard, she had come home to talk on the phone into the wee hours of the night, with Diana first, and then Lucy, who were both now worried about her the way she had worried about them all those years. Christmas was the hardest time, with Joe visiting in the afternoon and bringing each of the girls perfume and a sweater, but nothing for Maggie. They had discussed this already, on the phone. They would not keep up any charade about their roles, their relationship. And so, for the first time since 1969, they would not exchange gifts. She had bought a small artificial tree, although they'd always gone—as a family until the girls left, and then just she and Joe—for a real Norwegian spruce that filled the whole house with the smell of a forest. Instead Maggie bought the artificial one for the girls, who would be disappointed with no decorations at all. "Artificial" fit the mood perfectly. Set the tone. She had come to see the twenty-five years of her married life to Joe as just that: *artificial.* As she sat watching Lucy and Diana open their gifts, with Joe rocking from one foot to the other as he stood by the fireplace with a glass of wine, Maggie couldn't help but remember those first presents: He had given her a 1902 edition of poems by Robert Burns, a nice brown leather binding with gold letters—it was still in the glass case—and she had given him clothing, two shirts and a tie, because he needed new things to wear to his classes. And gray woolen gloves for the wet Boston winter. And then Christmas was over, and Joe was gone. She and the girls watched *It's a Wonderful Life,* although it wasn't. On Valentine's Day, when she deliberately stayed late at the library, browsing through the shelves of antiquarian books in the special collections department, she had come home to find roses on the front steps, left there by Larry the florist, who had an agreement with her about deliveries. "Just leave them on the step," she'd told him. Joe always sent roses to her on Valentine's Day, and on their anniversary. And she would never tell anyone that it had happened, not the girls, not Anita Wodehouse, who taught Dryden, Swift and Pope—bless her soul—she would never tell anyone that her heart had risen up at first sight of the roses, sitting sweetly on the front step as she swung her car into the driveway and caught them in her headlights. Roses from Joe! And she would never tell anyone about the lifelong journey she took down the cement walk, her heels clicking on the pavement like leaden raindrops, toward the card that was fluttering in the wind, fluttering along with the red ribbons tied around the roses. What would she do? If he redeclared his love, as he did every year at Valentine's Day, what would she say? Yes, come home, this old heart will heal. Let's let bygones be bygones. Let's run naked down Beauchemin Street. Let's take up again like young lovers, wild and crazy and sweaty in bed. Remember those fiery nights, blankets on the floor, sheets twisted beneath us? Let's do it! Let's do it all again! TO MOM, WE LOVE YOU MORE THAN EVER. DI &

LUCY, the card read. And before her heart could break, before the adrenaline of disappointment had time to rush throughout her body, she had thrown her head back and laughed aloud at the fool she still was. Di and Lucy. What would she do without her girls? The winds of March brought Joe's birthday, the Ides, on the fifteenth. Back in 1970, a quarter of a century ago to the day, she had bought him Gibbon's *Decline and Fall of the Roman Empire* as his first birthday present. He had always declared that one day he would read it, but the rigors of law school had never seemed to let up. When he finally began to practice in his hometown of Kansas City, he came home exhausted, carrying a briefcase bulging with papers that had to be studied for the next day's presentation. And so *she* had read Gibbon instead, the girls upstairs asleep, their homework neatly inside their books, Joe at work in his study, the sound of the grandfather clock in the parlor keeping up its steady tick-tock heartbeat. She had gone alone through thirteen centuries of human struggle, from the rule of Trajan and the Antonines to the capture of Constantinople by the Turks in 1453. Thirteen hundred years alone, never knowing that the day would come when nine months without Joe would seem even longer than any of that. She had read that Gibbon once noted that history is a record of "little more than the crimes, follies and misfortunes of mankind." Now, in the months since Joe had driven away from the brown Victorian, driven to Bridgette's little apartment by the university until he could find and purchase the condo in which they now lived, Maggie had come to see all life as such: crimes, follies and misfortunes. Mostly follies. The sixth day of April would hereafter be designated "McIntyre versus McIntyre Day," as their divorce came through with flying colors. On the last day of April, Diana's birthday appeared and disappeared in the Windy City, where she and Adam Fessler celebrated by visiting an Impressionists exhibit at the Chicago Institute of Art, followed with dining out on oysters and champagne. Just after midnight on May 5, Lucy, her firstborn, Lucinda Mary Patterson McIntyre, turned twenty-four on a windswept rocky pinnacle called Cadillac Mountain, on the coast of Maine, a birthday spent backpacking. That's how quickly it all happened. On May 20, anxious for the end of classes, Maggie had gone to the attic to search for the old paper on Yeats, and it was there that she realized there was a young woman everyone had forgotten about: her.

Joe had forgotten about her. The girls didn't even know her. She was Margaret Ann Patterson, who was—before she met and married Joe McIntyre, before she became a mother to Diana and Lucy—a product of the sixties. Maggie could remember the day her father arrived home early, carrying one side of a huge brown box while Mr. Giovanni, their neighbor, carried the other side. This event signaled the arrival of the Almighty Television, that gift from God to all baby boomers. It would be on this same television screen, this big gray-faced ghost that had moved into their lives, that Maggie would, at age fifteen, see John F. Kennedy's head blow up, and Jackie climb out onto the trunk in her little pink, blood-splattered suit to reach out a trembling hand for the Secret Service man. Then she would watch Caroline stand rigidly at her mother's side, while John-John saluted his father's passing coffin. Four years later, and out of the ashes of that first nationally televised tragedy, Maggie had found her first true love when she drove her blue Volkswagen up to Canada, to Little Bear Lake in Ontario, where she would work for three long summers as a waitress at the always lively Harvest Moon, where you could dance the night away if you had a mind to. An aunt who had vacationed there had found her the job, and looking back, Maggie now knew that those long tender summers at the Moon, all those days and nights spent with Robbie, had laid the foundation for the woman she might've become, should've become. That last summer, the summer of 1969, when she turned twenty-one, had been the best summer of her life. And then she had gone back to Boston, to get her master's degree, rereading Robbie's letters on the long nights when she couldn't sleep, admiring the nature drawings he had included with each letter, waiting to hear his mellow voice over a long-distance telephone line.

By then other events had changed the course of her life. It was also in front of that square-faced messenger from the gods, in the TV room of her dormitory, that Maggie settled down nightly on the sofa, between her two roommates, and listened as Walter Cronkite's soothing voice told them of the escalation of war in Vietnam. And then in her second month at grad school, in October 1969, she had to live through a brother dying in that war, when Douglas, "Dougie the Terrible," stepped on a live mine in the Mekong Delta and disappeared in body fragments. A boy who wanted to become a veterinarian because of his love for animals. This had changed Maggie, had broken the spell of youth, and she never again was able to retrieve it. With her heart mending from the loss of her only brother, she had found Joe, at the Boston versus UConn game in November; Joe, who became her substitute brother. She could see that now. Joe had been a replacement, a lovely comfort who even looked a little like Dougie, blondish hair, light brown eyes, more bookish than athletic. Joe filled up the void in her life that had materialized after Dougie's death. So what was she to Joe? Thinking back on it now, with all those spent years to give her perspective, Maggie realized that she was probably what many young, future lawyers would want in a wife, someone solid, someone versatile enough to tend to family and career and husband, that triumviral life so many women were just learning to lead in the sixties and seventies. And she was pretty. Joe must have seen that as an added bonus. Maggie had gotten out their wedding scrapbook the very day Joe packed his things and left, headed for a life of more Kodak Moments, this time with Bridgette. Looking at the wedding picture of the two of them together, Joe in perfect control with his arm protectively about her shoulder, Maggie was overcome with sadness. She looked more like his *possession* than his companion. Funny what one sees when that veil of youth has been lifted. They had worn jeans to their wedding, and sweatshirts that said BOSTON UNIVERSITY on them, perfectly suited for 1969. And now, twenty-five years later, there she was, trapped in a wedding photo forever, stuck there even after the reality of divorce, her soft brown hair curling about on her shoulders, her mother's legacy in the Irish nose and blue eyes, that defiant look on her face telling the whole world that this was the man for her, the life for her. And there had been love curled there, too, and passion, at least in those early days. So Maggie had sent Robert Flaubert one last letter, short, friendly, apologetic. She should have done better by him, done more, she knew that at the time. But she was living in a country at war, she told herself, and hardships happen. Losses. Fast good-byes. Whenever she could, she marched against the war, a picket sign trembling in her hand, Dougie's face on every soldier she saw passing by in airports, subways, restaurants. Her life filled itself up with busyness, cobwebbed itself against a lot of truths she wasn't ready to face. Several months after sending Rob Flaubert that dastardly letter, she and Joe were married.

Just a few years later they sat together upon their own sofa, in their new home on Beauchemin Street, with a three-year-old and a two-year-old tearing up the room, tearing up the silence, in front of their own TV watching hours of the taped Watergate hearings. Listening to speaker after speaker after speaker until, finally defeated, a tearful Richard Nixon had crawled aboard a helicopter that flew him up high above the turmoil, like Dorothy being carried to Oz, up and away from the perils of impeachment, from Washington, from a life he had dreamed for himself and Pat. And then it was time for another tragedy in her own family history, and this one was tough, even tougher than Dougie, when she had to live the filmstrip of her mother's death, the day a teenaged boy lost control of a snow-white laundry truck and met her mother's life head-on. Her mother had *lingered* for several days, although *linger* had never seemed an appropriate word to Maggie. It suggested a laziness on her mother's part, an absentmindedness, as though Mother had forgotten to turn off a burner on the stove. Maggie had later read that every day in the United States of America 87,000 cars and trucks are smashed in auto accidents. On July 17, 1985, a seventeen-year-old high school student did his patriot's share to keep the statistics accurate. Heavy-footed, anxious to outrace the awkward years of his teen age, a perfectly nice young man, his truck out of control, left the orbit of his life and entered someone else's. One laundry truck, and one 1982 Chevy Vega with a pine-scented tree dangling from its mirror, joined 86,998 other auto accidents that day. Still in a hurry, the teenaged boy died instantly, having no reason whatsoever to *linger*. Statistically, it was that simple. Emotionally, it would tear Maggie apart.

Three years later her father, to whom she had never been close, married a very nice, quiet woman named Vivian, who smelled perpetually of lilacs and always carried a small white handkerchief in her clasp purse. And now that woman was sitting down in Maggie's parlor, sipping from a cup of coffee, waiting with Maggie's father for a lift to the airport, knowing that Maggie was up in the attic rifling through boxes in search of some old paper. Not knowing that she had found the lace-bordered handkerchief—a treasure of which Vivian would approve. Not knowing that Maggie had had an epiphany, up there in the attic heat, at the top of the world, when she opened up a Pandora's box of memories and let Robert Flaubert's ghost finally escape. She had loved him for two long summers while she worked at the Harvest Moon. Maybe he was still there. Maybe time had spared him. Maybe the Harvest Moon was still blaring music out of its big square jukebox, the waters of Little Bear Lake lapping a few feet away from the wide, encircling veranda. She would apologize to Robbie in person, something she should have done twenty-five years ago. Maybe he had never married. Or maybe, like her, he had married and divorced. There were a million maybes, and all of them were wrapped up with that person she might've been, if Dougie hadn't gone to war, if Joe hadn't looked so comforting in his BU jacket, down on the bleachers in front of her, the wind doing nice things to his hair. Boston won, she now remembered, and smiled at the tricks of memory. Why would she remember such a trivial thing? She had gone for a beer after the game with Joe, who knew her roommate and came up to them to say hello. Joe had shoulders she could lean on, and now Bridgette was leaning on them. Bridgette was doing pirouettes on those shoulders.

This is what an epiphany can do to you: It can show you everything in perspective. Maggie would take a year's sabbatical. She would rethink her own path down life's highway, an opportunity her mother would never be given. An opportunity denied that teenaged boy. After all, she had money in her savings account. And she knew where she could get even more money, an action she should have taken months earlier, for her own sense of sanity. She put the lid back on the box that said COLLEGE PAPERS, the box that used to hold Robert Flaubert's love letters and the lace handkerchief he had given her, laden with his favorite cologne—*I want you to remember my smell*—the day they had stood by her little blue Volkswagen and kissed good-bye.

Down in the living room she smiled at Vivian, who was just depositing her starched handkerchief back inside her purse.

"Is that the paper you were looking for?" Vivian asked.

"No," said Maggie, "just some old letters I want to reread." She put the bundle of letters on the top of the glass case that held her precious first editions. The letters were first editions, too. She found her car keys on the coffee table.

"Ready?" her father asked, standing. He and Vivian had spent three days visiting from their home in Boston, the house in which Maggie had been raised, a house so full of memories of Dougie and, now, her mother, that a visit there only caused intense pain.

"Ready," said Maggie. She searched for her own purse beside the sofa.

"You look flushed," said Vivian. "All rosy-cheeked and healthy."

Maggie smiled. Was this Bridgette's secret? Get life by the horns before it gores you to death? Was this something that pretty Bridgette already knew?

"Oh, by the way," Maggie said, pausing at the front door to lift one of the suitcases. "Did I tell you that I've decided to sell this house?"

Common Loon

THE RETURN

April 30, 1968
Little Bear Lake

Dear Maggie. It's almost spring again. Some of the birds that went South for the winter are returning. I guess they're giving us a second chance. Did you see them fly over Boston? Did you hear their wings, late at night, as they flew by the light of the moon? I can't wait for you to take their example, and fly back to Little Bear Lake, in your little blue Bug.

It was late August, a time of glorious, impending color in Canada, when the leaves are thinking about changing hues for the year, hinting at what will come with flashes of bright yellow. Squirrels are still nut-gathering, and the geese fly in long sweeping V's in the sky, travelers leaving home for warmer climes. Maggie was flying against the birds this year, on the plane that carried her from Kansas City, up over the Mississippi River, and the flat farmlands of Indiana and Ohio, far above the industrial squalor of Lake Erie, and then across the western tip of Lake Ontario to land in Toronto. It was August 29, summer was curling up and dying beneath her, and she was going against the birds. Going against a lifetime of living.

Into a rental car she loaded two bulging suitcases and the heavily taped box that held those books she couldn't live without. She pulled out of Pearson Airport on Highway 400 North and prayed she would be able to find Little Bear Lake, considering the marks of progress she could already see in the landscape, buildings where none had been before, sharply paved roads, sprawling shopping malls. Later, when she knew what was what, she would have more books shipped, winter clothing, some paintings that were especially dear to her heart. For the time being, a storage house in Kansas City was holding the treasures that had once filled the brown Victorian house, had made it seem like home. Now the brown Victorian was on the market, waiting for new people to pamper it, with Joe and the real estate agent watching over things. "I'll call you as soon as an offer comes in that I think we can't turn down," Joe had told her. "I'll get your number from the girls." Maggie knew the deal would be a good one with Joe watching. Here was a lawyer with 50 percent interest in the outcome. Good hands. The same hands that took care of Bridgette. And then, when it was over and the house was gone, maybe she wouldn't have to hear Joe's voice again, at least for a long time, or see him stand around in the parlor looking at his watch, looking like the cat that ate the canary. She had passed through almost a year since the day he'd told her how his mature heart wanted to be young again, the way so many men of his generation wanted to be young. So they went hog-wild crazy, made fools of themselves for young women the age of their own daughters. Well, let them. Let Joe. Out of the ashes of their silver anniversary, which had arrived on June 21, the summer solstice in the northern hemisphere, Maggie had spent the day beside the backyard pool, sipping on a pitcher of margaritas, the radio blasting out songs on the oldies-but-goodies station. And that's how she had felt: an oldie but goodie. After that day, when it didn't even occur to her to look for red roses on the front step, after their twenty-fifth anniversary, the only damn special-occasion day she had left to live through would be the first anniversary of her divorce on April 6, 1996. Who knows? Maybe she would be celebrating Divorce Day on the shores of Little Bear Lake, where she had spent so many evenings with Robert Flaubert. She would sit on the little dock —if it was still there—with a bottle of fine red wine, a fine red sunset, the red eyes of the lake loons floating on the horizon of water. An oldie but goodie. "All I have to get through now is Divorce Day," she'd told Anita, who came by to drink her own share of margaritas beside the pool. "But what about Flag Day?" Anita had asked thoughtfully. "Shouldn't I come drink margaritas with you on Flag Day?" Maggie would miss her.

As she left Highway 400 the roads grew more narrow, until she was twisting around small lakes, heading across flat pastureland, then back into forests and hills. Hawks flew across dead hayfields, their flat broad wings shadowed on the ground below like small black planes. In the forests ravens swept above the tops of the evergreens in dark sweeping arcs. Maggie grew more at ease, feeling that old world peeling away behind her, across the border, in the very heart of America. She saw the sign first, before the building rose up in front of her eyes, a gray mountain of wood and stone ascending as if from an old dream. The Harvest Moon. It had been a quarter of a century, almost to the day, since she had seen it last, full of warm yellow lights and smelling slightly of the lilac bushes that grew along the north side each summer, the way Vivian smelled of lilac. Now here it was again, fallen into disrepair but still enchanting, gothic almost, with its second-story patio and double chimneys. How many Christmases had come and gone in wrappings and bows, happy times with Joe and the girls, while it sat here waiting? How many Kansas City rainstorms had caught her unawares? How many leaves had piled up on Beauchemin Street, marking each passing autumn? How many times had she corrected term papers? Brushed her hair? Bought pantyhose? Sent Christmas cards? All years that this small part of the world, at Little Bear Lake, had functioned without her, had spun toward its own future: THE HARVEST MOON. DINING, DANCING, COCKTAILS.

In its prime the house had been a showcase there on the lake, built by a lumber baron at the turn of the century, a wedding gift to his wife. But the couple had died childless and the home had passed through several hands until the last owners turned the downstairs into a rambling dance hall and bar, then opened its wide front doors to the public. But, to Maggie's dismay, even those prosperous days seemed to be over for the Moon. The windows were now mostly boarded up. Bricks that had fallen from the chimney lay on the ground like small red bales of hay. Goldenrod had claimed most of the backyard, and wild yellow mustard careened through what used to be the wide front lawn. There were trees, now, where she didn't remember them, fast-growing bushes that hid a portion of the lake from her view. And the trees that had been babies to her were twenty-five years older, growing toward their own futures. The porch had begun a slight sagging, a giving-in to gravity and to all those millions of footfalls that passed over it, some hers, some Robert Flaubert's. Dried grass and hay poked from areas beneath the eaves, indicating that swallows had taken up residence at the Moon. And, Maggie supposed, mice, too, were munching on articles of food that might've been left behind. Squirrels. Spiders. Well, at least someone, some*thing,* was still finding the old place useful.

Maggie got out of her car and slammed the door. Off in the distance, a crow called out, and then all was silent again. She hadn't realized until she made her feet move, made them carry her to the wide front door, that her eyes were watery with tears. How can time play such tricks? How can time be so *cruel*? She had always imagined that the Moon would wait for her, would encase itself in a gauzy cocoon of memory, and *wait.* And one day she would come back, as she was doing now, and it would open its arms to her, Brigadoon in the Canadian wilderness. But hadn't that centuries-old proverb taught her that *time waits for no man*?

"I guess I thought it would wait for a *woman,*" Maggie said. She stood now on the front porch, afraid to peer inside the window, afraid it might all have been a pleasant dream of youth and nothing more. No square old jukebox, no wide gray fireplace, no hardwood dance floor shining like a large yellow field. She thought she could smell lilac, but then, lilac only bloomed in the summertime, when the northern earth had finally shaken off winter and then the buds of spring. But in the autumn the smell was just as wonderful, that sweet perfume of woodsmoke, of burning rock maple, of winter hiding just around the bend. She had known that ageless smell of lilac for only three summers, while she worked her waitress job and spent her spare moments with Rob. She had heard the music of the fireplace for three sweet autumns, when in late September she had driven up to Little Bear Lake for the harvest moon dance, the last of the season. It was always during the autumnal equinox, when the *real* harvest moon was round and full and sweetly orange in the dark Canadian skies. During those times, the Moon's rock fireplace had seemed more like a second jukebox, such were the sounds it made of hardwood snapping and popping. Only three years, and yet those scents and sounds were burned, no, *branded* into Maggie's mind forever. She pressed her face against the window and there it all was, the long curving bar, the varnished pine-board walls, the wagon wheel chandelier—how they had laughed at that chandelier!—the wooden tables and chairs, now piled in one corner. Even the canoe paddles, which had belonged to Gil, the owner, were still crossed and on the wall behind the bar. It hadn't been the Copa Cabana, but then, no one had wanted the Copa Cabana on the shores of Little Bear Lake. That would've disturbed the loons. Instead, with its rustic decor, its huge heart of a dance floor, its friendly horseshoe bar, the Harvest Moon had welcomed rich and poor, young and old. It had been an earth mother, of sorts, a wilderness goddess. How many times had Maggie finished her night shift, counted her money, and then thrown off her sweaty blouse and skirt for a swimsuit so that she and Robert could jump into Gil's canoe and paddle out for a swim? Even at 2 A.M.! Or they would drive the twisty back roads, listening to their favorite hit songs filtering in over the radio, sitting in Robbie's pickup truck some nights as rain beat its fists against the metal of the roof. What would her mother have said, back in Boston, about those nights that Maggie and Robert Flaubert had taken a bottle of wine and paddled far out onto Little Bear Lake, where they could look back at the yellow lights of the Moon, as though it were a spaceship, the Mother Ship, and they were simply bobbing about in space until the time came to paddle back to her. That's what Maggie's last twenty-five years had been: a bobbing about in space. But at least she had paddled back to the Mother Ship with the girls in her life. She was not alone. She was just without a partner.

It was when she left the wide encircling porch and walked back toward her car that Maggie saw the sign. The wind had obviously blown it, tilting the post that held it, and now the sign faced the Moon, instead of facing the road and prospective buyers: FOR SALE BY OWNER, CALL 702-6642. Maggie looked at the lettering a long time, trying to put pieces of the past years together into a meaningful picture. The owners, when she knew the Moon, had been Gilbert and Maudy Clarke. They had seemed "older" to Maggie in those days, but in truth they were probably only in their late forties. Wonderful people. She had sent them a Christmas card for two seasons, until the girls began taking up so much of her time that her Christmas card list had shriveled up like a dying plant. (Robert Flaubert, out of deference to Joe, had never even made the list.) But Gil and Maudy—they'd be in their mid-seventies by now, if they were still alive. Could they still be the owners? That would explain why the dance hall had been closed down. It takes a lot of energy to run a bar, and even though Gil had been of good lumberjack stock, Maggie doubted he could keep pace with demanding tourists, and beer truck deliveries, and lugging cases of vodka around. Or maybe—and she hated to think of this possibility—they were both in Little Bear Lake Cemetery.

As Maggie jotted the number down on a piece of paper, a loon cried out tenderly from somewhere on the lake. She looked up quickly and saw it, floating like something made of foam, light and buoyant. The late afternoon sun caught its head and back, brought its velvety feathers to life. And then it dove, disappeared, and the lake calmed itself instantly, as though the bird had never been there.

Maggie smiled: she was back at Little Bear Lake. At least *it* was still here. What she needed now was a shower at that small motel she had passed on the drive in, farther up the lake—it hadn't existed in 1969—and a nice hot dinner. Then she had some phone calls to make, and some old voices to hear again.

As Maggie walked back down the driveway, a car appeared in the distance, its front poking around the turn in the road. It came toward her slowly as she stood, waiting. A face loomed from behind the steering wheel, another in the passenger seat, both staring, almost amused, the faces of an older generation. Maybe they assumed this foolish city person was looking for dinner at the Moon. Maggie nodded, and the car passed by. Then brake lights. Pebbles spitting up as it rolled backward and stopped before her. The driver leaned back patiently as his wife pressed closer to the window and looked up. Maggie studied them both. Their faces were like boots that have seen too much weather, too much scuff of life.

"If you're looking for food, dear, you need to go on down to Cindy's Cafe," Maudy said. She pointed back at Fort Wallace. "That's the closest."

"Thanks," said Maggie.

"The Moon ain't been open for three years," said Gil.

"I can see it's been a while," Maggie agreed. *Gil and Maudy Clarke!* They didn't remember her, but she remembered them. The last time she saw them, twenty-five years earlier, they had already started to look the way they would look for life. But when they'd seen *her* last, she'd been twenty-one. Her face hadn't yet settled into the more rugged looks of middle age. Her face hadn't been molded enough yet.

"We used to own this place," Gil offered, and then motioned sadly at the Moon. "But it just got too much for us to run."

Maggie nodded.

Now Maudy was peering up with a sudden intensity, a growing interest in this stranger. "Have we met before?"

"Yes," said Maggie. "We sure have, Maudy. A lot of years ago."

The look in Maudy's eyes shifted from puzzlement to sudden recognition. "Oh, my heavens," she said. "Oh, Gil, look. It's little Maggie Patterson all grown up!"

"Maggie?" said Gil, looking carefully at the woman standing before him at his car window. And then realization settled in. "Are you any more graceful with a tray of beer bottles?" he asked, smiling his toothy smile.

Maggie smiled, too. "Not much," she said.

"There must be something in the air," said Maudy, as she reached past Gil in order to squeeze Maggie's hand. "Guess who's home from Toronto?"

Maggie felt her heart do a little thump. Had Robert Flaubert maybe moved to Toronto? Would it be her good luck to arrive back in Little Bear Lake just as he did?

"Who?" she said.

"Claire," Maudy offered. "She's staying at her mother's."

The Great Blue Heron

RECONNECTION

May 2, 1968
Little Bear Lake

Gil and Maudy have begun work on the Moon so that it will be ready for next month's tourists. I've been putting in some long days of hammering and raking and carrying boxes. There are two good reasons for this hard work: (1) money, moolah, dough and (2) Maggie Ann Patterson will be coming back to work for the summer. I've raked up all the fallen leaves from our secret place. It's all ready now, and turning green with spring. Wish I had someone special to share it with. Know of anyone? Can't wait to hold you again. Love, Rob.

After thumbing through the few thin pages of the Little Bear Lake phone book, Maggie finally found the number she was looking for. There could only be one Luther Findley in Little Bear Lake, maybe in all of Ontario. Maudy didn't know why Claire was suddenly back in Little Bear, only that she intended to stay. And yet she had married, according to Maudy, and had children. So, had Claire been bitten by the divorce bug, like Maggie? The Clarkes hadn't mentioned Robbie Flaubert to her. She had waited for one of them to say something, and when neither did, she decided she wouldn't ask. She had broken his heart, and Gil and Maudy must have known that. Perhaps they were just too polite, felt the situation too awkward to bring up, and so Maggie said nothing. She would find out everything from Claire. If Claire had been back in Little Bear Lake for a week, she'd have had time to catch up on all the gossip. Funny, but twenty-five years can dissolve between two people and then, by punching out a few numbers on a magical piece of equipment, you can be reconnected to a voice from the past.

At first, Claire didn't know who Maggie was. All she knew was that it was someone calling with an aura of familiarity.

"I hate it when people do this to *me*, but can you guess who this is?" Maggie had asked when the voice on the other end admitted that it was, indeed, Claire Findley whose twin brother, Clarence, was the best cribbage player in northern Ontario. Maggie hadn't wanted to ask, "Are you the Claire Findley who worked as a summer waitress at the Harvest Moon?" She knew that putting a finger on the Moon would be a clue to Claire. After all, there hadn't been that many waitresses to come and go through the wide front doors of the dance hall. Claire would narrow it down to Maggie Patterson too quickly. So she asked if this was the Claire whose twin brother Clarence knew his game of cribbage.

"How do you know about Clarence?" Claire had asked.

"You'll have to guess who this is," Maggie continued. "I'll give you a hint. It's a voice from the distant past."

"Were you local or tourist?" Claire wanted to know.

Maggie thought for a minute. "I'll have to say tourist, if given those two choices," she answered.

"Oh, well, forget it then," said Claire. "Do you know how many tourists go through here in the course of one year? I'm talking Canadians, Americans, Martians. You did know, didn't you, that Little Bear Lake is now a hotbed for UFO sightings, or have you been gone too long? Well, it is. There's a UFO in every nook and cranny, in every pine and spruce. Of course, we all suspect that it's only Monty Whitburn, calling in fake reports. Monty's seen a few pink elephants in his day, too. By the way, you didn't say what planet you're from? Is it earth?"

Maggie smiled widely. Claire hadn't changed a

bit, not a quiver, in all those twenty-five years. Still wisecracking, and still, Maggie would bet, the life of any party.

"Well, then, let me ask you this," said Maggie. "Does Monty still have that old red Chevy, and does he still wonder who hid it in the hazelnut bushes down by the hockey rink?"

There was a pause on the other end of the line. Maggie could almost hear Claire's thinking mechanisms working on the details. They had sworn they would never tell another living soul about how they had hid Monty's Chevy from him. Only the three of them would know—the Three Musketeers—Claire, Maggie and Rob.

"Oh my Krishna!" said Claire. "Maggie? Maggie Patterson, from Boston?"

"One and the same," Maggie said. She could almost see Claire's pretty face, wondered if it had changed much in the course of so many years, if maybe she'd lost those freckles that had been scattered across the bridge of her nose.

"Oh, I can't believe it!" said Claire.

"Believe it," said Maggie. "It's me. And I still haven't told a soul about who hid Monty's Chevy."

"Hell, you might as well be from Mars," said Claire, "as far away as you've been gone for twenty-five years. God, but I have thought of you since that last summer, wondered so many times where you were. Just a couple days ago I told myself, Claire Findley, I said, you will live to see that woman again."

Maggie felt a stiffness in her throat, her chest. Why hadn't she at least written to *Claire*? Because Claire had been Rob's best friend, that's why. Somehow, cutting off Robert Flaubert had meant it was necessary to cut off his right arm, too.

"So it's Claire *Findley*?" Maggie asked, wanting to escape for the moment those facts about her disappearance into a new life.

"Long story," said Claire. "But I heard a long time ago that it's no longer Maggie *Patterson*. How's the hubby?"

"An even longer story, most likely," said Maggie.

"Well," said Claire, "I got a long time to listen. And it's only eight o'clock. We can drive over to Fort Wallace for a couple beers. Do you still drink beer?"

"Does Monty Whitburn still see pink elephants?" Maggie asked.

They met in Fort Wallace, at a small bar called the Lakeview, twenty miles down the road from Little Bear Lake. The Lakeview was called such because it sat at the tip of another lake in the beaded chain of lakes that sprawled across the Canadian timberlands. This was Crooked Lake, a smaller, less touristy body of water than Little

Bear. Claire had an errand to run first, so Maggie spent a few minutes driving along the twisting lake road, remembering those balmy summer evenings when she and Robert Flaubert would load a cooler of beer between them on the seat of his pickup, and then drive the gravelly back roads, the radio picking up the pop station in Toronto. They would end up at Robbie's secret, special place, across the cove from the Harvest Moon, a place where the soft green moss grew like a thick blanket in the summers, beneath shaded trees, with the water lapping up to the shore. And in the autumn, for that single week when Maggie drove up for the harvest moon dance, the moss would be brown and covered with dried needles from the towering pines. A secret and special place where she and Robbie had first made love. By the second summer, Rob had talked Gil into selling him a parcel of land there, which included the secret spot, and he had built a tiny dock as a surprise for Maggie, a private place for just the two of them. Some nights, after she had finally closed out the cash and said good night to Gil and Maudy, she would cut across the wide parking lot at the Moon and find the narrow trail through the woods, a trail that Robbie had blazed just for her, and she would go to him. It was always at the rise of the little knoll of fir trees that she could catch the sound of his music, songs from the pickup's radio, hit songs of the moment: "Leaving on a Jet Plane," "Honey," "Judy in Disguise," "Mrs. Robinson," "Hey Jude," "Love Child," "I Heard It Through the Grapevine," "Green Tambourine," "This Guy's in Love with You." That was Robbie, that last song, for he was head over heels in love with Maggie Ann Patterson. And she with him. Because there wasn't much privacy in the room Gil and Maudy had made for her, in their own living quarters at the Moon, she and Robbie always met at the secret spot. Sometimes he would wait for her on the wide front porch, and they would slip into his canoe and paddle away into the moonlight. Once, they hadn't waited to get to the cove, to the soft moss blanket. With the lights of the Moon blinking away in the distance like summer fireflies, Maggie had pulled her paddle out of the water and turned to look at him. This was how she had remembered him, all those years that his face came and went in her memory, came and went with the colored leaves on Beauchemin Street. She remembered him awash in moonlight, naked from the waist up, the moon on his cheekbones, on his hair, on his back; she remembered him touching her with silver fingers, on a silver night, the silver waters of the lake beating around them. That night of the full July moon. Sometimes, over the years, this memory would wake her, the way she used to wake with worry about the children. It would poke her awake, this silvery memory of Robbie Flaubert, and she would lie in the dark, on her street in Kansas City, in her state of Missouri, in the United States of America, next to her husband, Joe McIntyre, until that silver ghost of remembrance abandoned her and she fell back asleep, leaving Robbie Flaubert behind, in the gossamer moonlight on Little Bear Lake. He had joked that he was going to write his first book about that night. *It'll be a manual called "How to Make Love in a Canoe Without Tipping."* Had he become a writer after all? Sometimes, over the years, when Maggie went into a bookstore she would ask the clerk, "Are there any books in print by an author named Robert Flaubert?" And her heart would race as she stood waiting while the clerk read the microfiche film that listed books in print. Then the microfiche had disappeared and titles ended up computerized, and still no books by Robert Flaubert. Just Gustave, from whom Robbie used to pretend to be descended. The last time Maggie asked was in San Francisco, at an artsy little bookstore, when she had gone to Berkeley for a symposium on Ezra Pound. In the classics section she had spotted a poster of Gustave Flaubert on the wall. Beneath his sad, rigid face were the words *l'art pour l'art* (art for art's sake). And she had wondered again about Robert Flaubert, future Canadian author. When she had gone to the information desk and inquired, the clerk typed the last name, entered it, and then waited. "No, nothing by a *Robert* Flaubert," she said finally. "Do you know a title of any of his works? I can look for that." Maggie started to say no, but instead, a smile forming about her mouth, she said, "I believe he wrote a manual titled, 'How to Make Love in a Canoe Without Tipping.' " The clerk simply stared at her. "Or maybe I'm thinking of the movie," Maggie said, and left the store. That was seven years earlier. She had stopped asking bookstore clerks about Robbie. *L'amour pour l'amour*. Soon, she would know all the answers.

"I never dreamed the day would come I'd see you again," Claire said, after they'd hugged hello enough that people were stopping in the middle of private conversations to look over at them. They made their way to a booth in an area of the bar that was still empty. Claire dropped into the Naugahyde seat across from Maggie. She had put on a few pounds here and there, but she was still the same Claire, a smattering of freckles about her nose, a headband just like the bandannas she had worn in the sixties.

"You haven't changed a bit," said Claire. "You haven't even gained weight. That's not fair."

"I've got to run four miles a day," said Maggie. "And I read more ingredient labels on cans and packages than I do poetry these days. Watching the damn fat content. It isn't fun." Their beers arrived and they tapped the cold bottles together, in a toast.

"Here's to time," said Claire, "and old friendships."

"So what are you doing back?" asked Maggie. Claire looked at the Foosball players across the room, young men intent on winning, shouting out after each scored point.

"Want to hear the dull statistics?" she asked. Maggie nodded. "Well, I married a man named Charles Blakely in 1973," said Claire, "and I had two children. We were separated for a couple years and then divorced in 1985. I married another man in 1986, John Buck. That ended in 1987. We were both on the rebound, and you know what they say about that second marriage. Now, a smart chimpanzee would've been alert to the problems of this marriage thing by now, but guess what I did? In 1990 I went and married another man, named Christopher Dean, and I loved this one, Maggie, like back in those days when I first loved Charlie. And that should've been a clue to me, because he was *just like Charlie*. I used to say that Charlie even cheated on me when he was asleep, and it was true. I'd wake up at night and he'd be having a wonderful dream about some woman, a big smile on his face, his arms hugging his pillow. After years of that, the pain finally goes away and you're just glad it's over. But this last time around, it really hurt." She motioned to the waitress for another round.

"I'm sorry," said Maggie.

"My girls are both in college now," said Claire, "so I thought coming home might be a way to get the train back on the right track. There are good men out there. I just need to stop picking the bad ones."

"You have two girls?" said Maggie. "So do I."

"And you?" said Claire. "Why are you back here, at the ends of the earth?"

Maggie waited for the waitress to leave the beers and then disappear back behind the bar before she answered. "It sounds like I'm here for many of the same reasons you are," she said finally. "I've got a train off the tracks, too."

"Your husband?" asked Claire.

"Joe McIntyre," said Maggie. "He got up one day last year and told me all about the love of his life, who happened to be a twenty-seven-year-old paralegal in his law office."

"Jesus," said Claire. "Life can be such a barrel of crap."

"So," said Maggie, "I sold my house, and I took a sabbatical from my teaching job at the university. I have no idea what I'll be doing in a month from now, much less a year. I just know that I've got some loose ends to tie up. And Robert Flaubert is one of them."

Claire just sat and stared at her, the raucous voices of the Foosball players rising up in the background. "Robbie is one of them?" she finally asked.

Maggie nodded. Had she noticed something shaky in Claire's voice?

"Once I set things straight with him, once I tell him to his face that I'm sorry, I can start over again. And who knows. First loves are hard to destroy. Of course, if he's happy, that's another story. That's why I'm dying for someone to tell me about him. He was all I could think of on the flight to Toronto, on the drive up here." She knew Claire would know everything about Robert Flaubert. Small towns were still small towns, no matter how many years went by. Folks never lose touch with each other when they're born and raised in little communities, communities like nuclear families. Even if the lone member goes off into the world and never returns, he has left behind a mother, father, sister, brother, grandmother, grandfather, cousin, good friend, *someone* who knows his whereabouts. And that someone informs the community. You can never escape a small town. It's some kind of universal law. And Robert Flaubert and Claire Findley had been as close as brother and sister.

"Where is he?" Maggie asked, and she saw that Claire's eyes were glistening. "Does he live here? Is he married? He must be married. But is he happy? Did he move away?"

"Oh, Jesus," Claire said again. She took the beer napkin from beneath her bottle and blew her nose. "You really don't know, do you?" she finally asked.

"Did he ever ask about me?" Maggie wasn't listening. She had waited too long for answers. Claire's face had filled up with old memories now, and Maggie knew just what the memories were: they were of the Moon, its wide dance floor and big old jukebox and summer nights of skinny-dipping and sipping wine on the little dock and picking bowls full of wild strawberries and lounging in the sun while tourists poured into Little Bear Lake from all over Canada and the fifty states, memories of younger bodies and minds that were ready to take on the world, hearts that were pure, before divorces and stretch marks and those first strands of gray hair, memories of the Three Musketeers: Claire Findley, Robert Flaubert and Maggie

Patterson. Finally, Claire put the napkin down and looked across the table at Maggie.

"No, he never left town," she said. "He married a girl he met over in Coreyville. He married her in 1970. She was pregnant with their one child. Was he happy? I suppose he was as happy as any of us, given the stuff life shovels up now and then. I believe he came to love Julia very much. And he adored his son."

Maggie said nothing. There was too much finality in Claire's tone; she was finally hearing it for the first time since the conversation had gotten around to Robbie. "Where is he?" she asked softly, evenly. "Where is he, Claire?"

"I saw him last in 1990," Claire said. She was looking away from Maggie now, looking out the window in the direction of Little Bear Lake, as if she could still see Robbie there, that crooked smile on his handsome face, waiting, a picnic basket in the belly of the canoe, waiting for Maggie and Claire. "I had just come home for a visit, a month before I married Christopher. I wanted some of the peace that comes with being on the lake. So Robbie and I rented a canoe and spent a whole day on Little Bear. He was like the old Robbie. It was wonderful. Then I went back to Toronto. A week later Robbie was dead. A heart attack."

Maggie sat, stunned, in the booth across from

her old friend and tried hard to believe what she was hearing. All day, ever since she arrived in Toronto, and the closer she got to Little Bear Lake, she could sense him there beside her, could sometimes smell him in the smell of spruce and lake water, could almost feel him, the velvety surface of his skin, his fingers, his lips. *If he's married,* she'd kept telling herself, *I'll say hello and then I'll go away again. I'll leave him be. I won't try to do to anyone what Bridgette and Joe did to me. But what if he's not, what if he's not, what if he's waiting for me?* These were the thoughts that had been swimming around in her head all day. It had never even occurred to her that Robert Flaubert, who still looked just as she'd seen him last in that photo in her mind, might no longer be on the planet, might no longer be where she could talk to him, touch him. He was gone, lost forever, like the loon she'd seen dive earlier that day. He was gone, and the ripples on Little Bear Lake, the ripples he had caused by moving through the waters there, had vanished. It was now as if Robert Vincent Flaubert had never even been there.

"I've got to get out of here," Maggie said to Claire, and then she stood, her legs wobbly, and grabbed her purse.

"I'm coming with you," said Claire, but Maggie held a hand out.

"No," she said, "please. Tomorrow, let's have lunch. We can talk more then. But right now, right now, I need to be alone."

"Welcome home, sweetie," said Claire softly.

Autumn Leaves

THE LOSS

October 7, 1969
Little Bear Lake

Dear Mags. There's a light wind tonight on Little Bear. And just a sliver of moon over the cove. It's lonely in autumn, with everyone and everything gone, the leaves, even the geese. Sometimes, I feel like we've been left behind here, the way tourists leave behind things they no longer want. But then I remember the good times. And suddenly it's summer again, and the jukebox is blasting away at the Moon, and we're driving the back roads with the wind in our hair and life between us. You'll be back next summer, God's in his heaven, and all's right with the world. Love, Rob.

That had been the last letter he'd ever written to her. With it he'd sent a lovely sketch of autumn leaves scattered across the porch. A lonely picture. A day or two later, he would've received the letter from Maggie, with the Boston postmark, telling him it was over.

In her motel room, Maggie had arranged the huge bundle of letters from Robbie upon her bed, letters from the autumns, winters and springs they had spent apart after that first summer meeting in 1967. She had taken them out of her attic on Beauchemin Street and packed them safely into her little travel case. She had not been able, in all those years of safeguarding them, to reread them. Not able. And then, on the flight to Toronto, she had ordered a glass of red wine and then reached down between her feet and picked up the first letter: *September 9, 1967 . . . Dear Maggie. I miss you already. It's going to be a long winter and spring until you're back again. At least, you'll be coming in two weeks for the Last Harvest Dance. I want you to know that I meant it when I told you, the night before you left, that I love you. I'll always love you. You are the most incredible girl I have ever met. I dream of you at night. (I used to dream of playing hockey! Just kidding.) Claire says hi. Keep me safe in your heart. Rob.* And all the while she read, she was flying closer to him, flying closer to Little Bear Lake, flying back to the past with every intention of paying it the respect it deserved: the past shapes you forever. Respect she was too young and naive to understand a quarter of a century ago. She did not know, as she had whizzed past the Little Bear Lake Cemetery, the wind in her hair as it used to be on those wild and passionate nights, she didn't know that he was gone. A heart attack. Was it partly her fault? Can love gone wrong really break a heart in two, so that it never mends properly, even if it wants to? He'd married someone else, Claire said, and he'd seemed to love his wife very much. But there was something about how he died—a heart attack—that kept rising in her mind. All those long years, she had known this about her love affair with Robbie, had known what everyone back then knew: she had broken his loving heart. And now, that same heart had killed him. She would never tell him in person how sorry she was, how she had always carried that proverbial torch for him, all those years of family dinners, and baby diapers, and loose front teeth, and school homework, and graduations. She had carried a torch that would now have to be put out.

In her plain little motel room, with the lake beating away beyond her window, Maggie read the second letter Robbie had sent her, and then the third and the fourth, the fifth, read into the late hours of the night, piling the nature sketches he had put inside each envelope in a separate pile, sketches of flowers, and insects, and trees. She read the past, studied it, as though it were a history book you could pick up again and dust, find the page where you'd left off, and go back at it afresh. She read until she heard the birds of dawn begin to stir in the trees outside her window. It had all come back, the frantic, chaotic evenings of waitressing, the tourists sometimes fussy and rude, the big yellow dance floor packed with sweaty bodies, the tips piling up on her tray, the looks she'd catch from Robbie, from his usual stool at the bar as he waited for the night to end, and then the lake breezes upon them, flying with them into the night, flying with the night itself, time at their heels, time theirs for the taking, and Claire with her spirited laugh, all three hurtling themselves toward divorces and broken hearts and a modern world where they would never quite feel comfortable again.

She had promised Claire that she would be all right, that she just needed time to deal with the news, and that was true. She wasn't suicidal. After all, she still had two daughters to think about. But that fact didn't dull the pain of losing Robbie, losing him after being so close to him again, after twenty-five years. And now the only way she could feel him near was to reread the letters, in order, the way their love had unfolded, a day at a time. And so she read every one of the letters from the fall of 1967 to the fall of 1969, arranged all his sketches on the bed of the motel. In reading the letters again after so many years, it seemed almost as if everything was okay, was happening again, and she was moving toward her future, in control of it this time. Robbie was still alive and writing love letters: *June 4, 1968 . . . We've been working nonstop to get the Moon ready. Oh, yes, Gil gave me a raise last week. This is the last letter I'll write, for you will be pulling up to the Moon in a few days, in your little blue Bug, and I'll be a happy man again. P.S. You're cordially invited to The Secret Place for a huge surprise, and a bottle of wine. Love, Robbie.* The surprise had been that he had bought that little piece of land from Gil, the one that held their secret spot, and he had built the little wooden dock out into the water. She would go, tomorrow, and look for the spot, see if any of the dock was left. In the meantime, with the birds of dawn at her window, she cried until her pillow was wet with tears of regret. "I deserve this, I deserve this, I deserve this," she kept repeating, until she finally fell asleep. And there, in the strange little motel on the shores of Little Bear Lake, in the early hours of dawn, with his written words still swimming in her head, Robbie Flaubert came back to her, in her dreams. She saw him again, wearing his silver cloak of moonlight, as she turned in the canoe to look at him, his cheekbones magnificent, his naked skin the color of dimes, and then the two of them, rocking, the yellow firefly lights of the Moon beckoning from another shore, from the future, until they closed their eyes and the lights disappeared forever.

She met Claire at Cindy's Cafe, at noon, as she had promised.

"Jesus," said Claire. After all these years, it was still her favorite word. Robbie used to say that Claire was more religious than the nuns who had taught him in grammar school. *Not even* they *say "Jesus" that much,* he'd noted.

"Good morning," said Maggie.

"You look like hell," said Claire. "Didn't you get any sleep?" A waitress appeared with coffee and a bowl holding little tubs of milk.

"Are you eating?" asked Claire.

"A salad," said Maggie, although it was only the thought that she must put something in her stomach that propelled her to order.

"Mag, honey," said Claire. "I really thought that Gil and Maudy had told you about Rob. I wish there had been a better way."

"What would it have been?" asked Maggie. "There's no good way." She watched as the waitress wiped a table near the window and then arranged the jars of condiments. Finally she looked at Claire, steadily.

"Well?" asked Claire.

"I'd like to know," said Maggie, "I *need* to know.

Did he ask about me? Did he ever mention my name?"

Claire sighed heavily. It was obvious that Robert Flaubert was still a sore spot to her, too, and that she missed him greatly.

"He asked, all right," she said finally. "But you know Robbie. He never wanted anyone to know how hurt he was. He never wanted it to get back to you that he had asked."

Maggie smiled, sadly. That would be Robbie, his pride firmly on his sleeve.

"Your aunt—what was her name—you know she came back every summer for a few years."

"Rachel," said Maggie. "Aunt Rachel. She was how I heard about the summer job in the first place."

"Well, it was the same thing every year, as soon as your Aunt Rachel checked into her cabin. Robbie would come into the Moon while I was working, and he'd either wait until I got off, the way he used to wait for you, or he'd pull me aside so we could walk out onto the porch. 'Could you find out about Maggie?' he'd say. 'Could you ask where Mag is and what she's up to?' And I would ask your aunt. That's how we found out you'd gotten married that very next summer after you left. It was just four months after that, in October, that Robbie got married himself, when he found out that Julia was pregnant. And then, the next summer that your aunt came up, we heard you'd just had a new baby. Robbie had already had his son by then. He was two months old, if I remember correctly. Then, the second summer, we heard you had another baby. Robbie didn't really have to prod me to ask about you. I wanted to know, too, so I just went ahead and asked for myself and then filled him in later. He didn't want your aunt to tell you he'd been asking, you see. We even knew you'd married a lawyer, and were going to school again yourself. And then, one year, your aunt never came back again, just like you. And you might say our pony express ran out. Robbie built himself a nice home on the lake and set about raising his son. And I went off to Toronto and set about having a couple kids and a few marriages of my own."

"What happened to his wife?" Maggie asked. She was surprised to feel a warm flash of something—was it jealousy?—wash through her. This woman, this Julia, whom he had come to love, had spent all those years at his side, all those nights in his bed, under the silvery moon over Little Bear Lake, had borne their only child. But then, how could Maggie blame Julia? Julia had obviously known a good thing when she saw it.

"She moved back to Henderson Cove, about eighty miles from here," Claire answered. "That's where she was born and raised. Her family is all still there, and I guess it made her too lonesome to be here, knowing how Robbie loved this lake and all."

"His son?" Maggie asked. What would his child be like? How she wished Robbie could meet her girls, had even envisioned it on the long flight to Toronto. Had known he would see Maggie's own sense of humor in Diana, her sense of the studious in Lucy. What would his son be like?

"He's still here, still living in Robbie's house," Claire said. "I haven't seen him for several years. He was always out with his friends when I stopped by to say hello to Robbie. I hear he was torn up over his father's death. He had been in forestry school, Maudy tells me, because he wanted to be a forester like his dad. But then when Robbie died, he just dropped out of school, dropped away from his friends, keeps to himself."

"A forester?" Maggie asked, and smiled.

Claire smiled, too. "You know," she said, "Robbie probably could've become a writer. He was smart enough to write just about anything. But the call of the woods and the lakes was just too strong for him. You know that. He could never cut himself away from Little Bear."

Maggie nodded. Out on the lake, a couple were paddling their yellow canoe. On the opposite shore, a sprinkle of colored leaves was already boldly showing itself among the conifers. Smoke rose from someone's cottage, curled like a gray corkscrew in the blue sky. It was a picture made for Robert Flaubert. Maggie wanted badly to ask, *Did he forgive me, Claire. Did he ever forgive me?* But she couldn't. Not now. Not yet. She had risen in the warm autumn sun of that morning, her first morning back at Little Bear Lake in all those years away, and, her eyes puffy and swollen from tears, she had made a decision. Maybe later she would pry from Claire those most intimate details—*Did he ever forgive me?*—but in the meantime she would set about other things, things she could at least do something about. She ordered a second coffee.

"I guess you could say that I've been living Plan A for the last twenty-five years," Maggie said. "So, do you want to hear about Plan B?"

Claire looked at her with interest, nodded. "Well?" she asked.

"Well," said Maggie. "I'm gonna buy the Harvest Moon and open it back up. You better air out your dancing shoes."

Claire's face showed her surprise. "Are you kidding?" she asked.

"No," said Maggie. "I'm not kidding. I've already called Gil. We have an appointment with his banker this afternoon. It'll take a bit of time to finalize the paperwork, but Gil says I can start renovating now, considering we're friends. After all, I've only got about five weeks before the harvest moon. And I want that to be my opening night. I want to attend one more harvest moon dance before I die, even if Robbie won't be there. But the Moon will be a little different this time around. No dining. Just dancing and cocktails."

"I wish it had been like that when we were waitressing," said Claire. "Think of all that smelly fish we had to serve." She sat smiling, staring at Maggie from across the table, a Cheshire cat. Most likely she was running the image over in her mind of Maggie now in charge instead of waitressing.

"I'm placing an ad tomorrow for someone who can act as a kind of foreman," Maggie said. "You know, see what needs fixing up, order supplies, take charge of things. Gil's not up to that kind of work." Claire was smiling even wider now. THE HARVEST MOON: DANCING & COCKTAILS.

"Are you any better at carrying trays of beer bottles than in the old days?" Claire asked, the same question as Gil.

Maggie shook her head. "That's why I'll need a couple of good waitresses."

"I know you'll need a good bartender," said Claire. "So consider this an application submitted right now. While you were making money talking about Shakespeare, I was making money learning to mix the perfect Bloody Mary."

"Consider it accepted," said Maggie. They sat

for another silent minute, both watching the smooth waters of the lake, listening to the background chatter of the diner. The only thing missing was Robbie.

"Twenty-five years," mused Claire. "And here we are, back where we started."

"It's about time," said Maggie.

White-tailed Deer

RENOVATION

November 8, 1968
Little Bear Lake

Dear Maggie. There was another red sun tonight on the lake. This morning ice lay at the edges. The freezing process has started. Yesterday, just as the morning mist was rising over the lake, I saw two white-tailed deer drinking at the water's edge. And I thought of you, thought of us, and the curious way that the paths of our lives have crossed forever. It's lonely in Little Bear without you. Even those deer have each other. But I tell myself that spring will bring the thaw, and summer will bring Maggie. Hurry back. Love, Rob.

Maggie had arrived in Little Bear on Wednesday, five days earlier, and yet a world of things had already happened. The most important was the news about Robert Flaubert.

How would she forget him? How would she ever let him go, if she didn't breathe his air, sit by his lake, listen to his loons, and then, hopefully, exorcise him forever. And maybe, in the scuffle, she would discover who she was and what she wanted. Would she be a professor of comparative literature? Or would she be like "Gunsmoke's" Miss Kitty, tending bar night after night, waiting for Matt Dillon to finally kiss her? But Robbie would never kiss her again. Robbie was gone, like the migrating hawks, and he wouldn't be back.

She and Gil and Maudy had pressed onward, and once the bankers were satisfied with Maggie's financial statement, the Harvest Moon would be hers. The Moon hadn't been in bad shape at all, what with Gil and Maudy keeping it in fine repairs right up until they closed it, and then keeping an even finer eye on it from a distance. The repairs left to be done were mainly cosmetic, but were still bothersome considering that Maggie planned a grand opening on September 23rd, a Saturday which would also mark the autumnal equinox. That was propitious. The Moon had always celebrated its big harvest moon dance on Saturday night, which meant that it wasn't always on the equinox. But this year, in 1995, the equinox fell on Saturday. The moon would be at its fullest. With Gil's blessing, Maggie had gone ahead and run the ad for a sort of jack-of-all-trades person who could oversee repairs, order lumber, decide what else needed fixing. And then, when the work was over, he could remain as the Moon's general caretaker and handyman. The ad would run in *The Little Bear Weekly*, which would go to press on Tuesday, with papers delivered and on the stands by noon on Wednesday. In the meantime, she needed to get her personal life in shape. She had sold her car back in Kansas City, so she went ahead and bought a new one, a little green Firebird, perfect for her needs. Then, wanting to get the small upstairs living quarters in shape so that she could move out of the airless and cramped motel room, she and Claire had set about cleaning and painting and occasionally hammering. It looked as if a week's work would do the trick. Maggie had even contacted the small rug store in Coreyville to install new rugs and drapes, which they were happy to do in a hurry, autumn and winter being their off-season. She arranged her books on a bookshelf she found in one of the many antique shops in Coreyville and Fort Wallace. She bought beautifully framed prints—Manet, Monet, Degas, Pissarro—and hung them about the one-bedroom apartment. Actually, in Gil and Maudy's day it had been a two-bedroom, with Maggie sharing the small extra room in the summers. But now it was a one-bedroom, with the extra room being turned into a small study. Maggie bought a cherry desk and lamps and a thick Persian rug and set about making the upstairs apartment as cozy as she could. How many nights had she lifted herself in the darkness from her bed, Gil snoring soundly next to his wife in the other bedroom, and stared down at the lake, at the little cove with its sturdy dock which waited only a quarter of a mile away. Those were the nights when she'd been too tired after work to spend time with Robbie, and so she had gone up to bed, exhausted, only to find herself waking, inexplicably, in the middle of the night, sensing that he was at their special place, waiting, watching. So she would rise in the balmy night, pushing aside the sweaty blankets to stand at the window, the perspiration on her body turning chilly with the lake breeze coming in at her, goose bumps forming on her neck, arms. But she would stand there until she heard the faint hint of music wafting upon the lake, from the pickup's radio, Robbie listening to those hit songs he loved so much. And sometimes, if the moon was bright enough, she would see him there, his silhouette on the dock. Once, lightning lit the sky, and it lit Robbie, too, the outline of a person in love with Maggie, in love with the lake and the trees and the sky, so much in love that he longed to stay among them, beneath them, near them, every second he could. A man filled with the passion of nature and love, this Robert Flaubert. *There's such a thing as too much time spent on the lake,* Maggie would tease him. *No, there isn't,* he always answered. Now

Maggie was back in the small upstairs apartment, making it fit for her special loves and interests, art and books, and there would be no more music coming from the dock.

On the very first day she returned to the Moon after deciding to buy it, she had stood on the wide veranda and looked, finally, at where the dock used to be. It was still there, still looking sturdy with time, still letting the lake lap about its posts. But she wasn't ready to go there, not yet. Seeing it from her old bedroom window, now her study, brought too sharp a stab of memory. It just wasn't time. So she set about making herself a living place above the Moon and hoping that she could make the Moon itself ready for a grand opening.

It was on Tuesday night that she and Claire decided that the little apartment was as cozy and livable as it would ever be. The addition of plants from the nursery in Coreyville gave the place an air of homeyness, and Maggie was ready to settle in. As soon as Claire left, dog tired and ready to go home and get some sleep, Maggie lit scented candles, filled the small bathtub with hot water and bubble bath, and sank down into the suds. Then she found her favorite pair of flannel pajamas and pulled them on. Already the evenings were beginning to grow chilly, but she would sleep with the window open, in order to hear the waters of the lake. At least for a little while, until she tired of reading. She would close it before she fell asleep. But that didn't happen. She must have dozed off about eleven, because it was almost 1 A.M. when she woke, her book upon her chest, the chill of the lake seeping into the small bedroom. And that's when she heard it, music, music coming from somewhere off the lake. Maggie felt a tremulous shiver rush up her back, along her spine, along her arms, a tingling vibration. Music from the lake! She moved to the window and there, with her ear pressed against the screen, she heard it again. Soft ghostly music, wafting toward her. Pop music, it sounded like. Her heart was beating rapidly, so chilling was it to awaken to the same sounds of all those years ago, Robbie and his music. Then she felt anger. Who was playing music at this hour? Anger was followed by amusement, and she smiled. How many forty- and fifty-year-olds had opened their cottage windows and were distressed to hear Robbie's radio, on all those long-ago summer nights? All a matter of perspective. She closed the window, but in her heart was a heaviness that kept waking her on and off for the whole night. When the first light of dawn rose up around the lake and then crept across her bedroom window, Maggie finally fell into a deep sleep.

It was the sound of the phone ringing at ten o'clock that woke her. She had planned to be up by seven, back at work downstairs in the Moon by eight! She stumbled out to the tiny kitchen and put some coffee grounds in her Mr. Coffee. While it was perking, she quickly washed her face and brushed her teeth. In her study she pushed the replay button on her answering machine. It was Claire. "Call me the instant you get this message!" Claire had said. "You won't believe who I just ran into. Oh, where are you? Okay, call. It's urgent." And then there was a click. Maggie went back to the kitchen for her first cup of coffee. Just as she was about to return to the study and phone Claire, she heard the sound of an automobile. From the kitchen's window, she looked down on a dark green pickup truck pulling into the driveway of the Moon. Claire would have to wait a few minutes. Besides, Claire was always all drama. Maggie went down the stairs that led up to her little apartment. She heard the pickup's door slam. She turned the corner of the building, into the driveway, and stopped dead in her tracks. She felt the coffee cup falling from her hands, hot coffee splattering about on the ground. She felt the world spinning beneath her, everything she knew and believed falling away.

"I'm still asleep," she whispered, "I'm still asleep and this is a nasty dream." It was Robert Flaubert, standing before her, as real as flesh and bone. Robbie. He smiled, and Maggie felt a cry rise up in her throat, a cry of pain, a cry of joy. *Robbie, dear Robbie.* He was bending now to pick up the broken coffee cup.

"Did I frighten you?" he asked. Maggie could say nothing. It was Robbie's smile. It was Robbie's voice, his brown eyes, eyes so dark they appeared black. It was his black silky hair grown long and over the collar of his shirt. Robbie in faded jeans and cowboy boots. "I just stopped by to talk to you about the job offer." Robbie's long tall body. And yet, this was the Robbie she remembered from all those years ago. This couldn't be the man who died of a heart attack, at the age of forty-six. And then she knew. "I'm Eliot," he said, and reached out a hand. "Eliot Flaubert." For a long time, she said nothing at all. This was Robbie's child, this replica of himself, this handsome young man, Robbie's blood and bone. Flesh of his flesh. *He named his son Eliot!* This was what kept running through her mind. *He named his son Eliot.* How many nights had they chosen names for the children they might one day have? Robbie was always joking about it. *If it's a girl, we'll call her Robbie, Jr., to make her tough. And if it's a boy, we'll call him Eliot, after your favorite poet. Because with a name like Eliot, he'll learn to be tough.* Maggie stood, electrified, still unspeaking, gazing at the young man before her, a hand now to her eyes to shade the sun away.

"Eliot?" she finally said, her legs rickety beneath her, and he nodded. And Maggie remembered, suddenly, all those nights in Robbie's truck as they rode along the wooded back roads, drinking wine and letting the wind spray against their faces, remembered how she loved to recite T. S. Eliot, her favorite poet. *Let us go then, you and I, when the evening is spread out against the sky.* She and Robbie had chased the sun down in his old pickup truck, tore up the back roads with music blaring all the way from WPTR down in Boston. And then they had sat with nothing but silence between them, listening to the waters of Little Bear Lake as it rippled forward, ahead to the future, and then Robbie's cool hand sliding beneath her blouse to clasp her warm breast. *Let us go through certain half-deserted streets, the muttering retreats of restless nights . . .* "I don't wanna hear from Mr. Eliot right now," Robbie would whisper, his lips warm and soft as feathers against her neck, the wild sound of night birds rising up around them in the blackness, and between them only the raw pumping of blood in their veins as he pulled his jeans down and kicked them off, threw off his shirt, while she slipped her panties down and pushed her skirt up around her waist. Cotton against skin. Mr. T. S. Eliot forgotten about for the time being. And then the feel of him pushing into her, pressing her back to the sweaty vinyl seat, her fingernails trying hard not to hurt his back. And then the fire, the burning in her stomach that she would never find with Joe. *I shall wear white flannel trousers, and walk upon the beach. I have heard the mermaids singing, each to each.* He named his son Eliot! "Eliot?" she said again, and he nodded.

"I really did scare you," he said, "and I'm very sorry. I guess you aren't used to visitors yet, considering you're still not open." And then he smiled, Robbie's smile, the crooked one that meant he was only half serious. "I'm hoping the job is still available, for the jack-of-all-trades foreman you're looking for."

Maggie nodded. "It's still open," she said. And then she realized something. "How'd you know about it? The paper isn't out until noon."

Eliot handed her the pieces of broken cup and then brushed his hands on his jeans. He may have even beat his father on height. Maggie guessed that he was probably six feet two. Robbie had topped off at six even.

"I met an old friend of my father's at the café about an hour ago," he said. "She told me."

"Claire?" asked Maggie, and Eliot nodded. Maggie remembered the phone message. *Call me the instant you get this message. You won't believe who I ran into. It's urgent.* "She told me you were his friend, too," Eliot continued. "And that you three used to have a lot of fun together."

Maggie was finally recovering from the shock—she would kill Claire—enough to put her hand out to Eliot. He took it in his own hands, big hands, like Robbie's, strong and durable, hands that can carry a canoe over a long portage, hands that had come down from a long line of woodsmen, pioneers, sturdy stock. Yet the skin was as soft as deerskin in Maggie's own hand.

"We were very good friends," said Maggie. "And we miss your father a great deal. I had hoped to see him again. I didn't know about . . ." She stopped. Eliot had begun to fidget, the toe of his boot kicking now against the broken shards of coffee cup, a tinkling noise. Maggie realized that she was treading upon fragile ground. "If I had known you were looking for a job," she said, changing the subject, "I could've saved myself the price of an ad."

Eliot smiled. "What is Ed charging these days?" he asked. "Two bucks? Or has it gone up?"

Maggie laughed. "See how much I need a good jack-of-all-trades?" she said. "Ed must've seen me coming a mile off, city slicker that I am. He charged me five bucks."

Eliot smiled his crooked smile again, his dark eyes sparkling. "You'll make it up next summer," he said. "Ed always plants too many tomatoes and cucumbers. If he overcharges somebody, they just wait until the tomatoes are ripe and they stop by Ed's house for a little chat. You'll get it back in lettuce alone." Maggie felt an inexplicable warmth rise up in her heart, standing there in her old jeans and bare feet and talking to Eliot. It was Robbie's wit alive in him. *Robbie alive.* He was peering at her with such intensity that Maggie realized she must look like some crazed woman. Had she even brushed her hair? She reached up a hand to touch it and found the quick ponytail she had made on her way down the stairs. And the Missouri State sweatshirt that she was wearing was covered with blotches of the blue paint she had used in the tiny bathroom. What must she look like, standing there without makeup? Without *shoes*, for crying out loud? Yet Eliot seemed to approve of her appearance. "Claire says you're turning into a regular country girl," he added, and pointed down at her bare feet, amused. "That's a big compliment here in Little Bear, considering you're a bona fide city slicker."

"Well," said Maggie. "Even in Boston, I was the Girl Scout from hell. The job is yours, Eliot. Now do you want a cup of coffee?"

He shook his head, smiled another of his half smiles. "Are you crazy?" he asked. "I can't stand around drinking coffee all day. I've got work to do. Claire says you expect to open this place on the harvest moon." And, with that, he turned and walked back to his pickup, his long tall body moving with the same sure stride that Robbie had had. From the truck's window, he called back to her.

"Is it all right if I set up a charge account for you at Bagley's Hardware and the Little Bear Lumber Yard? They'll trust you if I tell them it's okay."

Maggie nodded. And then she stood there in her bare feet, still wishing she could have that first cup of coffee, and watched as the dark green pickup truck drove away in a flurry of dust.

Sparrows

WALLS

November 30, 1967
Little Bear Lake

Here's the list of "Most Played Songs on Gil Clarke's World Famous Jukebox." This is thanks to my own endless flow of quarters, of course. And now, I've got Maudy playing them, too, because they remind her of "the good old days," all except for the Doors, which she hates. "It's too smutty," she says. "Music is eternal, Maudy," I tell her. "Smut is ageless." Maybe one day she'll come around. Needless to say, I had to have the records specially ordered in Coreyville, all except for the Doors. I'll try not to wear them out before next summer so that you can hear them, too.

1. Blue Moon (Boy Wants Girl)
2. Some Enchanted Evening (Boy Meets Girl)
3. Stranger in Paradise (Boy Falls In Love With Girl)
4. You Send Me (It Gets Serious)
5. Light My Fire (Real Serious)

"You're ordering these records for the jukebox?" Claire asked. She'd been reading a list of things which needed doing, a list Maggie had made and presented to her. Now, her eyebrows arched, she was staring thoughtfully at Maggie, waiting.

"That's right," said Maggie. "You see a problem with that?" She went back to varnishing the shelves behind the bar. Outside, Eliot could be heard giving instructions to two roofers he had hired to repair a damaged section of roof. All in all, the Moon was looking like a new beast, shipshape, rejuvenated. Gil and Maudy had stopped in earlier to take a quick look at how things were progressing and they had left glowing. "It's almost like the old days," Maudy had said. "All you children back again." Claire had laughed heartily at this. "We've got just a few years left until we kick fifty, Maudy," she said. "We're hardly children." But Maudy was undeterred. "Still," she said, "fifty seems young to me these days, and all this bustle taking place, and with Eliot here and all, well, it *is* like the old days." And then she and Gil had crawled into their car and puttered away.

"It's just that I find this an unusual list of records," Claire was now saying. "I mean, 'Blue Moon' by the Marcels? 'You Send Me' by Sam Cooke? 'Some Enchanted Evening' by Ezio Pinza? 'Stranger in Paradise' by Tony Bennett? They aren't exactly current."

Maggie stopped varnishing and considered Claire for a moment. "You know how Gil let everybody order their favorite songs, so that they'd always feel special when they played them?" she asked. Claire nodded. "Well, that's how I want our customers to feel. We've got plenty of room to put a lot of current songs, too."

Claire folded the list and put it inside her jacket. She said nothing for a moment, and Maggie hoped that this was a sign that it was all over. But it wasn't. Claire cleared her throat, a little too loudly it seemed.

"Maggie, sweetie," she said, "are you sure you want to do this to yourself? Do you think I don't know that this is a list of Robbie's favorite songs, from when he first met you? I had to listen to Robbie play the jukebox in here so much that I can tell you the lyrics to all these damn songs, even today. And I can tell you the ones he played when he found out you weren't coming back, too. But what good would that do? And what's it gonna be like for you, hearing those songs again, here at the Moon, of all places?"

Maggie put the lid back on her can of varnish. When the shelves were dry, she would stock them with glasses. "Where else should I listen to them?" she asked. "Besides, that's just his list for 1967. It could've been worse. He sent me 1968 and 1969, too."

"But why do this?" Claire asked. "Why tear yourself up? Isn't it bad enough that we got all these memories of the Moon to deal with? And now there's Eliot, looking like a damn ghost. Why make it worse?"

"Aren't you going to be late?" Maggie asked. "I thought you had an appointment to get your hair cut. Oh, by the way, tell them at Radio Shack that I'll pay whatever it costs to FedEx the records." She looked questioningly at Claire, who simply raised her eyebrows again and shook her head. Just before she disappeared out the front door, Maggie called out to her. Claire turned and waited.

"If they can't order 'Some Enchanted Evening' by Ezio Pinza, tell them I'll settle for Jay & The Americans." Claire probably raised her eyebrows again, but Maggie turned away before she could see. She heard Claire telling Eliot something in the front yard, and then her car drove away. Maybe Claire was right. Maybe she shouldn't be pushing the knife in so deep, but reading Robbie's letters night after night was bringing it all back to life. How could she tell Claire, *I want it back as close as it can be. That's the only way I'm ever going to get over it. Get over him.* This was the journey she'd set out to accomplish, after all, this expedition to the past, this fact-finding mission to antiquity. And if she came out of it more hurt than when she went in, then that was a hazard she had to face.

"I want you to see something," she heard Eliot say from his stance in the doorway. She turned slowly to look at him. For five days now, ever since he had come into her life, she found she could not turn to face him quickly, for if she did, her breath would catch in her throat and she could say nothing until, finally, the shock of seeing Robbie in him wore away. She turned slowly whenever Eliot approached and asked her a question, or informed her that he'd discovered something else that needed fixing. She turned slowly, telling herself as she turned, *This is Eliot. This is not Rob. This is Eliot.*

"What is it?" Maggie asked. She wiped her hands on the bar towel and then tossed it aside. Eliot was wearing faded jeans and a black T-shirt. So like Robbie. And the way he did his work, with slow perfection, was Robbie's way. At times, Maggie felt as though she were in a study project, the adult woman given a chance to rethink the young Robert Flaubert, analyze him. She had known years ago that he was special. But it was only as a woman who has seen a chunk of life that she came to realize that Robert Flaubert had been more than special. He was like some kind of unicorn in the deep Canadian woods. She could see just how rare he had been by watching that same rareness in his son. But she was observing from a safe distance, keeping Eliot at bay, sending Claire to conduct most of the discussions of repair work. As much as she wanted to get to know Robert's son, she had kept a near visible gap between herself and him. It wasn't just that he reminded her so of his father. There was something else that unnerved her: Eliot seemed to know her, treated her with such familiarity that one would think they had been acquaintances for years. And during loose conversations, in the days following his arrival, casual moments in which the whole crowd—Eliot, Maudy, Gil, Claire and Maggie—bantered away the hours as they painted and hammered and swept, Eliot had said things that startled Maggie. Once, when Maudy was teasing Gil about taking her to an opera in Toronto, just one time before she died, Maggie had joined in on Maudy's behalf. "You should take her, Gil," she'd prodded. Eliot was surprised at this. "Why?" he asked Maggie. "You *hate* opera." When Maggie asked how he knew that, he shrugged. "Just a lucky guess," he answered. And then there was the dress Maggie had given Claire to drop off at the cleaners in Coreyville. Eliot had come inside for a glass of water just as Claire was folding the dress over her arm. "Blue," Eliot said, nodding at the dress. "Your favorite color." Again Maggie had asked, *How?* "Because your eyes are blue," he answered. "That simple." And when Claire had made a casual comment about something being *as overrated as Shakespeare*, Eliot held up a finger to his lips. "Careful," he said to Claire. "That's Maggie's number one man." Maggie had reflected on this. It was true that she considered Keats to be her favorite poet, a post formerly held by T. S. Eliot. But she always maintained that Shakespeare was far above every other writer of every age. He was above that *number one* on the list, existing in a realm of his own. And she had said this often, over the years, in discussions with friends and students. But she didn't remember saying so to Eliot. "Because you're a professor of literature," he had answered her. "Don't they *all* think that?" Well, maybe they did.

"What do you want to show me?" she asked now, as Eliot leaned in the doorway and waited.

"It's a surprise," said Eliot. "Come see." They walked side by side, down the wide driveway leading up to the Moon. The early September day was magnificent. Across the road, where a small field lay along the edges of heavy forest, a crow called out from the top of a high tree, its lookout. Out on the lake, gulls cried, their swooping wings sweeping the blue sky. Squirrels scurried across the ground, bearing hazelnuts for storage. Goldenrod was as yellow as it would get, and now the leaves of the trees had begun to burn, were turning bright orange and red. This was nature at her best. This was a living, breathing landscape, getting ready for winter, getting ready for the long white battle, and Robbie was part of the land, part of the water, the sky, the trees. Robert Flaubert was everywhere.

"There," said Eliot, and pointed. They had stopped just at the end of the drive, at the entrance leading into the Moon. Maggie smiled.

"Oh, Eliot," she said. "It's lovely."

"I thought it might be nice to put that stone wall up again, the way it was," he said. "I used to play on that wall. When I was little, I thought it was ten feet high."

Maggie nodded. It *was* lovely. He had rebuilt the small stone fence that once edged the front of the property, for twenty feet or so on each side of the driveway, and three feet high. Many of the rocks had fallen off the wall and were lying in the grass, moss-covered. Eliot had rescued them all, cleaned them, replaced them, and now the wall looked just the way it had when Maggie pulled up to it on a June day in 1967, a coarsely drawn map in her hand from Aunt Rachel. And she had sat in her little blue Bug and stared ahead, beyond the wall, at the Harvest Moon, a huge rambling creature that hugged the shores of the bluest lake Margaret Ann Patterson had ever seen in her entire life: DINING, DANCING, COCKTAILS. The little stone wall was back.

"Thank you, Eliot," she said, and she turned slowly to look up at him, the cry suppressed in her throat. There was sweat on his forehead, small drops of perspiration, and she almost reached out and brushed them away. But then she remembered. "It looks as good as new," she said. He nodded.

"I had to move a nest out of one of the openings," he told her. "But it was abandoned, so I guess it was okay." Maggie smiled. Robbie used to stop the pickup truck for small frogs crossing the road, for large moths flying toward his lights, for snakes slithering onto the tar. *They're all alive,* he'd say. *Who am I to decide their time is up?*

"I know what you mean," said Maggie. "Claire knocked down the swallow nests under the eaves of the Moon without telling me. I don't suppose I could've left them, but it would have given me pause as to what to do. That's so much architecture. So much work." Eliot seemed to be listening intently.

"Did you know," he asked, "that in the eighteenth century, people thought that swallows spent the winters at the bottom of ponds? How else could they survive, what with all the insects they eat either dead or hibernating? No one ever imagined that they could fly over eleven thousand kilometers, all the way to Chile and Brazil and Argentina. When I see them coming back in the spring, I think of all the places and things they've seen that I never will." Maggie could listen no longer. This was Robbie, telling her about nature, teaching her about the planet. *If we don't learn all we can about Mother Earth,* he'd pointed out, *how can we make it a better place, protect it for the next generations?* This was Robert Flaubert talking, this discourse on swallows.

"Thanks again, Eliot," Maggie said. "It was a wonderful idea to mend the fence wall." And then she turned away. She knew he had wanted to talk, had sensed in him a need, right from the very beginning. Maybe he knew about her and his father. Claire didn't tell him, but had Robbie? Was this why Eliot seemed to know so much about her? And did he want to find his father in *her*, too, as she had in him? Maggie walked slowly back up the long drive leading to the Moon.

"Wait till Maudy sees the wall," Eliot shouted after her. "She'll want me to run for mayor." Maggie stopped, halfway up the drive, and looked back. In the autumn sun his black hair shone like a crow's wing. He was sitting on the wall now, his long legs thrust out before him, crossed at the ankles, that crooked smile on his face. She would have known that he was Robert Flaubert's son had their life paths crossed in any city airport, in any dimly lighted restaurant, in the heart of the busiest subway station. It didn't take the shores of Little Bear Lake to tell her that this was Robbie's blood and bone, walking, talking, living. She knew it intellectually, as a matter of genetics, for we carry in our blood the blood of our ancestors. It's not something we can see, but it's there. We carry in our bones part of their marrow, and on those bones we are clothed in skin, the cells of which partly belong to them. Eliot's blood was 50 percent Robert Flaubert's blood. Eliot's lips were part Robbie's, his eyes, his hair. *This is simple genetics. Nothing more.* Maggie smiled at this handsome young man lounging in the warm September sun that enveloped them.

"If Maudy wants you to run for mayor," she said to Eliot, "then I suggest you do it. With Maudy on your side, you'll win."

"Hey," he shouted, "you look just like that actress—what's her name?—she won an Oscar for some movie."

Maggie smiled.

"I hope you're not referring to Joan Crawford," she said.

"Do you know how this Canadian sun lights up your hair?" Eliot asked now. "It would never shine like that in Missouri."

Maggie turned and continued walking up the wide driveway to the Moon, knowing, all the time, that his eyes were on her, watching her as she had been watching him, for nearly a week, from behind the new window panes of the Harvest Moon.

It was early evening, when everyone had finally gone for the day and Maggie was alone, that she decided to find the old trail through the woods. This was the one that Robbie had blazed for her so that she could scale the little hill behind the restaurant, and then walk the quarter mile around to the cove and to the special spot. It had stopped being the "secret" spot once Robbie built the short dock that ate its way out into the water. Claire had told her that Robbie had built his own home, where he had lived with his wife and son, at the opposite end of the lake from the Moon. Maggie wondered if old memories compelled him to do this. He had, after all, loved the upper cove, and the tiny dock, the birch grove. As far as Claire knew, the land there still belonged to Robbie. Now it was time for Maggie to go look, see what was left of the memory. So she pulled on her oldest jeans, knowing that the brambles just before the hill might tear at her legs, and she donned her long-sleeved flannel shirt as protection for her arms, and she went like an explorer, out of the door of the Moon and into the late afternoon sun.

At first, the trail seemed to stop, its way blocked

by a hoard of bushes—chokecherry, Maggie thought—that had grown across the path. But Maggie found alternative trails around the most cumbersome of obstacles, one of which was a fallen tree with branches still reaching to the heavens, and she finally managed to scale the small hill that would now lead her down to the special spot. It was at the crest of this hill that she usually heard Robbie's incessant music, but not this early September evening. Instead, she heard the caw of a distant crow, and the raucous gulls in their ceaseless quest for food, and the lonesome wind stirring up the crisp red leaves of the white birches that grew around the cove. No music. Just the wing-beats of memory fluttering near her ears. And then she was descending the hill, the path there still most visible, used almost, and she was pushing past the sumac and into the grove of white birches. And there it was, the mossy blanket, now turning brown with autumn, still stretching beneath the thickly growing birch trees, a spot only eight feet by eight feet, protected by overhead leaves until the autumn rains took them away. But in the summer, in the glorious summers, those birch leaves had rattled above their heads like wonderful coins, keeping the sun away from the mossy spot, holding up the rain the best they could, keeping away the winds. Maggie stood, staring. It was still there, nothing growing up out of nature's heart to reclaim it. The mossy spot was still there, and it was so clean it looked as if it had just been swept by a large broom. The way Robbie liked to have it, before she arrived. And now she was back, and the special spot had remained untouched for a quarter of a century. How was that possible? Her answer came when she made her way to the little dock. It was still as sturdy as ever. Newer boards here and there, one or two looking only a summer old, told that repairs had been done over the years. And there, floating in the water near the post closest to shore, still hidden in trees, was a six-pack of beer. A nail had been driven into the post and the plastic beer holder had been slipped onto the nail. A natural refrigerator, considering how cool the waters of Little Bear Lake were, year-round. Someone was keeping this place alive, someone was keeping it up, as though it were an apartment complex, or a city park, a garden, maybe. Someone was keeping an eye on things, and Maggie suspected that it was Eliot Flaubert.

That night she slept fitfully, as she had done her first night in Little Bear Lake, the night she learned that Robert Flaubert was no longer among the living, but out among the spruce and pine and lake waters: wherever it is that the departed go when their physical bodies tire of the earth. She slept fitfully, her dreams bringing to her the face of that first true love, a love that never died out, Robbie's face. But this time, when she turned to him in the canoe, there in his cover of silver moonlight, she could tell something was different about him. His hair was longer and resting upon his shirt collar, his face a slight bit thinner, his smile a bit more mischievous. It was Robbie, but it wasn't Robbie. And even in the thick gauze of her dreams, she knew. "This is Eliot," she heard herself say, the waters of the lake lapping up around them, and then she reached out in the silvery night to touch him.

Jukebox at the Moon

SOME ENCHANTED EVENING

March 13, 1969
Little Bear Lake

Dear Maggie. I feel so very alone tonight, one of those feelings that come quickly and are difficult to explain. I got to thinking about Pop, and how we used to go on canoe trips when I was a kid. And then one day, when I was ten, he just paddled away somewhere and we never saw him again. (Actually, he got into his 1953 green Chevy and drove away, like some kind of movie star.) In 1960, we found out he had died in a car wreck. I tried writing something down on paper tonight. It's supposed to be good for the soul, you know. But it didn't work. So I got in my canoe and I paddled out into the middle of the lake. At times like that, I need to see all around me, so that nothing can creep up and catch me unawares. Back on shore, I saw the lives of my neighbors and friends, lives lit up in the lights of their homes, their own cocoons and dreams and nets of safety. For some of us, there is no net, and I don't know why. I don't mean to talk about all this, but at times, I feel as if the only safety I've ever known is with you.

There was less than a week to go before the harvest moon dance. Work had come along magnificently. Maggie had hired Gil and Maudy part-time, someone to oversee orders and deliveries and those small need-doings that only folks who have worked for years in a business know about. Beer and liquor trucks had been pulling up to the Moon. Maggie had decided to serve simple hors d'oeuvres for the grand opening, to make the event most special, and now Claire was busy running back and forth, picking up items at the bakery in Lakeview and the massive Loblaw's grocery store in Coreyville, storing up for the event. Maggie had advertised in all the surrounding small town newspapers, all the way to Coreyville. The Moon was still the only dancing establishment for miles around, so it would seem like a good investment, considering that Gil hadn't wanted an arm and a leg. And you could trust someone like Gil when he told you what was what with the property. You could trust him unless you were Joe McIntyre, lawyer. Maggie had come in from painting the trim around the front porch to discover Joe's voice on her answering machine. Would she call him, please, it was important.

Maggie considered this. It was important? Perhaps Bridgette's face had broken out with nasty pimples? Maybe she had graduated from her training bra and Joe needed advice on cup size. Actually, Maggie knew that the call was about the brown Victorian, for Joe had said so. There was a buyer willing to meet their price. So she phoned him back, expecting to talk about the house. But then Joe, having heard about her purchase of the Moon from Lucy, had gone on to offer his opinion of the whole thing. He was dubious, he said, about this business venture of Maggie's, asking his lawyerly questions about demographics, building appreciation, and so on. Maggie had stopped him. "Joe, I'm returning your call because you say the house on Beauchemin Street has a buyer at our price. This is the only business we need to discuss. And since the buyer is meeting our price, all you need do is send me papers to sign. There's a Federal Express office in Coreyville. Now, is there anything else I need to know?" There wasn't. Good. Then let him worry about his own demographics. She could have said some of the snide things she had thought, but she didn't. The life she had led with Joe McIntyre was now floating somewhere over the American Midwest, floating like a diaphanous cloud over Kansas City. A rain cloud, maybe. That was all. Maggie went back to what she had been doing before she got Joe's message: arranging for several radio advertising spots on the Coreyville radio station.

By Tuesday, just four days before the grand opening, the Harvest Moon became officially Maggie's. After several trips to Gil's banker in Coreyville, after numerous phone calls and neat financial statements, it was final. And *finality* seemed to set the tone at the Moon as well. The roof was finished, in perfect condition again. The big dance floor still needed to be painted and then varnished, but the rest of the place was in shape. A band from Coreyville had been hired, one well-recommended by locals. Fred's Electronics, from Lakeview, had been by earlier to work on the massive jukebox and now it was playing again, and would be kept busy Saturday night, during band breaks. Fred suggested that Maggie buy a modern jukebox, one that played CDs, but neither Maggie nor Claire liked the idea. They would keep the old one, at least let it audition itself for one more season. Then, if the multitude—meaning the current generation—wanted to oust it by popular demand, so be it. Maggie's special record orders still hadn't arrived, but Eliot, who had gone to Coreyville for a new water pump, promised to stop by the Radio Shack there and check to see if they were in. Currently on the jukebox were records from when Maudy and Gil were still running the Moon.

"Okay, Cinderella," Claire said to Maggie, who was on her knees packing boxes of straws beneath the bar. "We need to celebrate the fact that you, Maggie Patterson, former waitress, now own the best damn dance hall this side of, well, *somewhere.* But it's important that we celebrate it." Looking up from her boxes of straws, Maggie agreed. It had been a long day of work. They had eaten quick sandwiches for supper, and then finished unpacking the new glasses, lining them on the newly varnished shelves behind the bar. Now it was eight o'clock, and it seemed like a good idea to stop work for the night. There was just the two of them left, so Maggie got them cold beers and plopped them onto the bar. Then she found a bar stool and slumped down onto it. Her feet had begun to hurt. Claire was at the big jukebox, already pumping quarters into the thing and searching for selections.

"I like the notion of records on a jukebox," said Maggie, watching Claire make her selections. "Instead of CDs."

"Me, too," said Claire. "But Fred's right. If you want the younger crowd to play the thing, you'll need to at least order some new records. I told Eliot to select a bunch. I hope you don't mind." Maggie shook her head. She was thankful that

Claire had thought of it. She'd been too busy concentrating on signing those final papers.

"We'll christen the fireplace tomorrow night," Maggie said. "It's getting cold enough for a big fire in the evenings." *If you make a fire for the dance,* Maudy had cautioned earlier, *it may get so warm you'll need to keep all the doors and windows open. And then there's body heat to consider. But I've seen a few harvest moon dances when it was so cold that we kept the fireplace full all night.*

"Hey, girl," said Claire. "Do you realize how hard we've worked these past few days?"

Maggie nodded. "And there's still lots to do," she said.

Claire looked at her with those famous raised eyebrows. "Simon Legree, will you cut yourself, and me, some slack?" she asked. "Relax for one evening. We still got almost a week before the grand opening."

Deciding that Claire was right, Maggie tilted her beer back and drank a quick drink from the bottle. Claire pushed a couple of buttons on the jukebox, and the music started, a song Maggie didn't recognize.

"Eliot asked me today why you avoid him," Claire said, quite suddenly, and it caught Maggie off guard. She started to argue, but then resisted. Eliot was right, and she knew she couldn't fool Claire.

"It's just still so difficult," she said.

"It's like looking at Robbie, all over again," said Claire. "It's like listening to Robbie. 'Twilight Zone' stuff."

Maggie nodded. "And it seems as if he *knows* me, Claire," she said. "Is memory genetic, for Chrissakes? Did he inherit Robbie's memories of me?"

"Apples don't fall far from the tree," said Claire, as though she were delivering the answer to an exam question.

"Thank you, Sir Isaac Newton," said Maggie, "for that scientific rendering." But she still couldn't shake the feeling of Eliot's occasional remarks, his all-knowing stares.

"Hey, look at this!" said Claire, not concerned in the least with Eliot's psychic abilities. "Maudy's still got Percy Faith's 'Theme from *A Summer Place*' on here. I wonder if there are any grooves left on the record at all."

Maggie frowned. "Please don't play it," she said. "I'm too tired for any top-notch memories tonight."

Claire finished her selections, and now she took her bandanna off and tossed it onto the bar. She took a sip of her own beer. She looked at Maggie with amusement. "You can never get away from the sixties," she said. "Will you tell me why that is? I mean, you hear of people getting away from the fifties all the time. Shit, people *run* from the fifties. The forties. Even the seventies. But you can never get away from the goddamn sixties."

"Maybe only those of us who came of age back then think that," said Maggie. She was admiring the varnished shelf behind the bar, now lined with sparkling glasses ready to use.

"Maybe," said Claire. "But one thing's for sure, we were a generation of lovers who listened and believed and lived by the words to songs. I know every generation is, to some extent. But remember, we had all those political songs, those antiwar songs, and I think we paid more attention than kids do today."

"What the hell did you just play?" Maggie asked. The old jukebox was booming.

"Mötley Crüe," said Claire. "I thought it would keep us from falling asleep here at the bar."

Maggie nodded. She had become somewhat acquainted with Mötley Crüe when the sounds of their music blared from beneath Diana's closed bedroom door. It would definitely keep two women in their mid-forties from falling asleep at a bar.

"You know," said Claire, "I sometimes feel that my whole life history can be charted by what was on the pop charts at the time the largest events in my life happened. If my children ever get interested in genealogy, I can send them to a damn *Billboard* magazine."

Maggie smiled. It was so good to be watching Claire's face again, seeing the quirky little way she pouted when she was being particularly thoughtful. It was so good to rediscover the friend in her.

"Okay," Maggie said, "I'll bite. Using songs, give me a little of your history that I missed out on. We still haven't talked much about ourselves. I think we're reacquainted enough, don't you?"

Claire nodded. She lifted her Miller Lite. "And there's nothing like a cold beer to speed up the reacquainting process," she said. "Well, let's see. In 1972 I was feeling real good about myself because Gilbert O'Sullivan had just released 'Clair,' and my oh my, when that song came on, I glided across floors. An entire song written for a girl named Clair."

"I remember that song," Maggie said.

"How could I not fall in love after such a boost to my ego?" Claire wanted to know. "I had just met Charles, so I was ready. And then my fate was pretty much sealed by the lines of Roberta Flack's 'First Time Ever I Saw Your Face,' which is lucky, when you consider that another big hit that year was 'My Ding-a-Ling.' " Maggie laughed heartily. It occurred to her that this was the first time she'd really laughed in a long, long time.

"I'd forgotten about that awful song," she said.

"But you know what," said Claire. "I can't even hear that goddamn 'Ding-a-Ling' song without having my heart and mind fill up instantly with fondness, and I'm singing along, thinking, 'Oh, I love this song,' before I remember that I don't. I *hate* that song. But what it does is remind me of a time and place when I was in love with Charles, innocently in love. And for a moment, it's all back, the sweetness of that memory, of my young heart." Claire patted the side of her bottle with a bar straw.

"It's true," said Maggie. "We all do it. I sang along to 'Rubber Duckie' just the other day."

"It's too bad," Claire continued, "that Tammy Wynette hadn't released 'D-I-V-O-R-C-E' in 1972. I might've been spared what turned out to be the agony of Charlie. I married him in 1973, and I was pregnant with Holly in 1974, and guess what the hit was that summer, when I was seven months pregnant? Paul Anka's 'You're Having My Baby.' Do you know that I still love that song to this day until I remember how much feminists are supposed to hate it."

"Are you a feminist?" Maggie asked mockingly.

"I think so," said Claire. "Anyway, the very next summer, I was pregnant with Jessica, and the big hit was 'Love Will Keep Us Together,' by the Captain and Tennille, but I knew then that it wouldn't. I knew then that even with suspenders welded to him Charlie couldn't keep his pants up when I wasn't around."

"I'm sorry," said Maggie. She pushed some of Claire's straight brown hair back behind her ear. "That stuff is never easy to live through."

Claire shrugged.

"So, by 1976," she said, "I was thankful for songs like 'Disco Duck.' I didn't have to think. All I had to do was find a good baby-sitter for after the kids went to sleep, so that I could go out once in a while, like Charlie had been going out, and I could drink a couple beers and think about those nights at the Harvest Moon, with you and Robbie, when Robbie used to play classy songs on the jukebox, like the songs on that list you gave me, 'Some Enchanted Evening' and 'You Send Me' and 'September in the Rain.' "

Maggie grew suddenly solemn. They *were* classy songs. The other guys used to tease Robbie, but he didn't care. She could see him again, his tall body swaying across the dance floor, all by himself, waltzing about to 'September in the Rain,' as Claire and Maggie sat on bar stools and laughed at him.

"Robbie used to say that loving a good song is like going to a good psychiatrist," Maggie said, and Claire nodded in memory. "It'll probably do you more good, and it'll certainly cost you a lot less." They were silent for a minute, remembering him, remembering how he loved words and music, how songs transformed him.

"My whole damn life is like a big record album," Claire said finally. "Side A is *before* I met that Charlie and had my wonderful kids. Side B is *after* I met Charlie and had my wonderful kids."

"You're starting to sound like one of those made-for-TV movies," Maggie warned.

"And what about you?" Claire asked. "Tell me about Joe taking up with that little paralegal." Maggie felt tension suddenly in her stomach. She was just trying to find the right words to tell Claire, without hurting her friend's feelings, that she simply didn't want to discuss Joe, when the sound of an engine turning into the driveway caught her attention.

"Listen," she said, a hand cupping her ear. "I've been saved by the crunch of tires."

"I'll take a rain check," said Claire, "but I'm all ears about this little paralegal. And remember, I've got a lot of experience when it comes to The Other Woman Syndrome. The important thing is to retain your dignity. For instance, never ask her where she buys her clothes."

A car door slammed out in the driveway and Maggie turned on her stool to look. "Gil must be back for another inspection," she said.

"You know," Claire noted, "with Gil peering over my shoulder the way he does, I'm beginning to understand how Gomer Pyle must've felt around Sergeant Carter."

Maggie laughed. She was just about to shout, "We're in here, Gil!" when Eliot appeared in the doorway, in jeans and a pale yellow T-shirt and brown cowboy boots, a beer in his hand. He leaned against the doorjamb.

"Ladies," he said, "can I interest you in a ride around the lake? The moon is coming up, and I think it's in our best professional interests to get out there and make sure it's starting to turn full for Saturday night."

"Hey, handsome!" Claire called out to him. "Get over here and get yourself a fresh beer." Maggie tried to answer, but she was struck with his outline there in the door, leaning like he owned the world around him. How many times had she seen Robbie lean that same way, in that very same doorway?

"I solved the beer problem already," said Eliot. "It seems to me that three hardworking adults could share a single six-pack and a cool relaxing drive. You've been in here all day long, and you'll be inside a lot more than that before your careers as bartender and club owner are over. So come on. Let's go taste some nature."

Claire was putting her bandanna back on. She nudged Maggie. "I told you," she said. "No matter how hard you try, you can't seem to get away from the sixties. Let's go." She tweaked the end of Maggie's nose as she passed by. "Get the lead out," Claire added. And so Maggie found her feet moving, the way they did in the old days, tired from an evening of fast work, but going toward Robbie and a night on the lake, or at the mossy place, or on the back roads, another living, breathing night with Robert Flaubert. But sometimes it had been she and Claire and Robbie, those "Three Musketeer" times, when Claire had no date, and so the three of them ganged up together against the night. Maggie's feet moved out the door, past Eliot's tall lanky frame, Eliot himself smelling of shaving lotion, his muscled arms tan from the roof work he'd been overseeing. Maggie went out and climbed into the waiting pickup, and with Claire in the middle, the three of them flew off into the coils of the past.

They talked about Robbie just a little, with Claire bringing him up. Robbie was still a soft subject to Eliot, too. But he had heard about the Three Musketeers from his father.

"You guys must've been something," he said.

"We were," said Claire. "Did he ever tell you about the time we stole Monty Whitburn's Chevy and hid it by the hazelnut bushes down by the hockey rink?"

"Claire!" said Maggie, and nudged her. "You weren't supposed to tell!"

"No," said Eliot, "I hadn't heard about that one."

"See?" asked Maggie. "Even Robbie didn't tell." Eliot laughed. The wind was rifling his hair, and occasionally, Maggie stole a glance at him, his perfect profile so like his father's, one elbow out his window as he drove.

They circled the lake that way and ended up again at the driveway to the Moon.

"Another time around?" Eliot asked.

"I don't know," said Maggie. "We really should be getting back. It's been a long day, and we've got so much to do tomorrow."

"Will you listen to yourself?" said Claire. "Where did you lose the spirit, woman? In that university classroom? The night is young!"

"There's the moon," said Eliot, and pointed. And there it was, indeed, climbing up over the mountain on the opposite side of the lake, looking almost full, though it would be Saturday before that happened in fact. But to the eye, the orange ball that was climbing up into the evening sky was nearly spherical.

"It's breathtaking," Maggie admitted.

"I know what," said Eliot. "Let's not drive the lake again. Let's just go down by the water and watch the moon rise." The women followed him. The lights were still on inside the Moon and, from the water's edge, Maggie looked back at the building with great satisfaction. It had been, and would be, hard work. But it was a wonderful feeling, a better feeling than standing before a class of twenty-five students, only one or two of whom were truly listening—*listening*, not just taking notes for a test. This was a kind of self-satisfaction that Maggie had never felt before, and she liked the feel of it. She liked the feel of Claire and Eliot and Maudy and Gil around her, the bustle of people who seemed more like family than Joe ever did. Than her own father. It was true that, since her mother and Dougie had died, and since the girls had left for their own lives, that Maggie was feeling like the perpetual orphan. And her father, well, he was the person to whom one sends special occasion cards, and telephones on birthdays and Christmases. But the truth was that, ever since he had married Vivian, albeit she was a wonderful woman, he had become Vivian's husband, and he had stopped being Maggie's father. There was nothing to forgive of this. He was managing his own life the best way he could. And now Maggie was doing the same with hers.

"My dad used to take me fishing on this lake," Eliot was saying now. He nodded at the expanse of water, to the opposite side where the moon was rising. "If you had binoculars," he said, "you could see our house—*my* house—over there. It's a reddish brown."

"So is the whole mountain, reddish brown," said Claire, her hand shielding her eyes.

"We miss him a lot, too," Maggie heard herself say. She turned and looked up at Eliot, into his black eyes, and then she reached out and touched his arm, squeezed it. He looked back at her with such intensity that she felt her face flush, in the cool evening air.

"He was an original, all right," Claire said. From far out on the lake, the loons called out with their haunting, melancholic music.

"They'll be migrating any day now," said Eliot. He bent and found a small rock, which he skipped gently across the surface of the water.

"I'll hate to see them go," said Maggie. She felt exuberant now, floating in a way, looking back at the lights of the Harvest Moon as it sprawled among the trees, sprawled almost to the water's edge. "Let's have a nightcap on the patio," she announced. "It'll be a bit chilly, but we're tough. Besides, we can each have a cognac, to christen the Moon, and that will keep us warm."

"Perfect idea," said Claire. "I knew the old Maggie would show up sooner or later. Remember what I told you, kiddo. You can't outrun the sixties."

Maggie went up to her small apartment for two sweaters. Eliot had a sweatshirt in the truck for himself. Claire was to pour three cognacs, and everyone would meet on the screened-in veranda overlooking the water.

"Where's Eliot?" Maggie asked, when she returned with the sweaters and found Claire sitting alone.

"He said he had to get something from his pickup that he'd ordered for the bar," said Claire. "He'll be right out." They wrapped themselves in sweaters and sat staring at the waters of the lake. The moon seemed more orange as it rose, the evening sky growing darker around it.

"If you weren't real careful," said Claire, "you would think we had stepped inside some kind of travel machine. I don't even feel that extra twenty pounds tonight."

Maggie laughed. "We could *market* that kind of time machine," she said. "The Time Warp Diet." Eliot appeared from the bar and joined them on the veranda.

"Ready for a toast?" he asked. He lifted his cognac, warmed it in cupped hands. Claire and Maggie did the same. The three glasses came together, and they waited.

"Well?" asked Claire. Eliot thought for a minute.

"Here's to old friends," he said, and they nodded. "And here's to the best damn fisherman, woodsman, guide, philosopher, sometimes writer, and all-times father, that ever lived." Maggie felt her eyes grow moist, but she mustn't let Eliot see this. Claire had told her the local gossip, about Eliot's hard time following his father's death, his dropping out of school, dropping away from his friends. Maggie had come back to tell Robbie she was sorry, to make up for lost time, if it was possible. Well, it wasn't possible. So, maybe helping Robert's son would be the next best thing. He would want that of her. Of Claire. They clinked glasses.

"Here's to Robert Flaubert," said Maggie. "Descended from the great French writer, Gustave Flaubert."

Eliot laughed. "He used to say that even then, huh?" The women nodded.

"Here's to Robbie," said Claire, "and here's to this reunion, of sorts, of the Three Musketeers." They drank from their glasses, their hands and the tips of their noses chilly, the gibbous moon flying like a lost balloon over Little Bear Lake.

"Tell me something, Eliot," said Claire. "If it's not too personal, that is. Have you ever been in love?"

Eliot laughed, shook his head. "Love is like absolute zero," he said. "It's only possible in theory."

"But," Maggie countered, "haven't scientists recorded temperatures one millionth of a degree above absolute zero? That's pretty darn close."

"Close is only good in horseshoes," said Eliot, and he smiled at her with that lopsided Flaubert grin. "Who wants to get close to love? Either it's the whole basket, or nothing at all."

"You two are getting too technical for me," said Claire. "I asked a simple little question about love, remember?" She finished the rest of her cognac quickly. Maggie was about to ask if she wanted another, but Claire interrupted her. "Oh hell," she said. "What time is it?"

"Only a little after ten," said Maggie. "Why?"

Claire bounded up. "Listen, you guys," she said, "I'll see you tomorrow. I promised my mother I'd pick her up at Bingo, which is over at ten."

"You're late," said Eliot.

"Naw," said Claire. "Mom and her friends stand around outside the school gym for fifteen minutes after each Bingo night and talk about how the ladies from Coreyville cheated."

Maggie smiled, but she felt instantly uncomfortable. She had just gotten used to the notion of Eliot there in Robbie's stead. But she wasn't ready for Claire to leave. Claire rubbed the top of Maggie's head as she passed by.

"Save me a cup of coffee in the morning," she said. "Make six cups instead of two." And then she was gone, the screen door of the veranda slamming behind her. Eliot waved her out the door. He turned to Maggie and smiled.

"Was she always such a whirlwind?" he asked. Maggie nodded. They sat for some time, watching the moon, listening to the last of the night birds, seeing the occasional outline of a great blue heron as it traversed the lake in search of its night roost. The air grew more chilly.

"This has been a very special night for me," Eliot said, finally speaking, there in the darkness, on the other side of the veranda table from Maggie. "I've never felt so close to my dad since, well, since he died."

"You must miss him terribly," said Maggie, and Eliot nodded.

"I miss him as a son would," he said, "but I miss him as a friend, too." Maggie could understand this. She herself missed Robbie in the same way. A rare combination, that. Joe McIntyre, she had finally come to realize, had never been her friend.

"How's your mother taking it?" she asked. She no longer felt that subtle little jealousy she had felt earlier about this woman, Julia, whom Robbie had married. Now that she'd met Eliot, all that had vanished. Julia must be an extraordinary woman.

"She couldn't stand to be near Little Bear Lake anymore," Eliot said. "It's better for her to be with her mother and father again. They're getting on in years. And it was time for me to live on my own anyway."

Maggie considered this. According to Diana and Lucy, he was more than old enough to be on his own. Eliot was twenty-five, and after all, the girls had left home at twenty-one and twenty-two. But girls were always more ready than boys to fly the nest, weren't they? Yet Maggie wondered why everyone was in such a hurry. Maybe it was best to stay with your natural-born pack until it was absolutely necessary to head off across the savanna. Surely this was the way nature had intended it. Cro-Magnon teenagers didn't just get up one day and strike out across the open terrain alone.

"This is getting depressing," said Eliot. "How about another cognac, boss? One for the road. If you think I've had too much, I'll just swim home." He bobbed his chin at the opposite end of the lake. Maggie laughed. It was true in Little Bear Lake that locals often drank a few beers as they circled the lake on evening drives, especially on the dusty back roads where a passing car was rare. Barry Fleck, the local sheriff from Little Bear, just reminded folks to be careful.

"I guess I can trust you for one more," said Maggie.

"How 'bout at the bar, Miss Kitty?" said Eliot, in his best western twang. Maggie agreed. It was growing chilly on the veranda.

She poured them cognacs at the bar, and then joined Eliot on the stool next to his.

"Tell me something," he said. Maggie sipped at her cognac, trying hard not to meet his eyes. She felt that discomfort again, the discomfort she had felt the minute Claire left, an urge, almost. She knew now what it was, the truth behind the uneasiness: she wanted desperately to reach out again and not just touch him, but to hug him, to hold him close to her.

"What do you want to know?" she asked.

"I want to know why you're avoiding me," Eliot answered. "For more than a week now, I've had a hard time getting you alone in one place to say a single sentence to you."

Maggie shrugged. "There's been so much to do," she said. "I guess I've been single-minded. Preoccupied." Eliot reached out and placed his palm over hers, a warm hand, and Maggie felt an instant shiver run up her arm.

"It's because I remind you of him, isn't it?" he asked. She said nothing for a time. Outside, through the screen door leading onto the wide veranda, she could hear the autumn wind pick up, tree leaves rustling, the lake waters slurping the shore.

"Yes," she finally answered him. "You do remind me of your father. Very much." He squeezed the hand beneath his.

"Another toast," he said, and lifted his cognac. Maggie raised her own, and touched it to his glass. "I consider it an honor that I remind you of Robert Flaubert, but here's to us, here's to *now*." They drank to this toast, and then his mood lifted, the somber Eliot flown away, and in his place was the witty, jocular Eliot. How many times had Maggie seen Robbie do this? Go from pensive and introspective to suddenly mirthful? The two faces of Janus.

"Your father used to own a piece of land," Maggie said. "Just down the lake." She pointed in the right direction. "There's a dock still there. Who owns it now?" She was surprised to hear herself mentioning the special spot of land, the little dock. The cognac, the moon, something must have eased her inhibitions.

"I own it," said Eliot. He watched her closely as he said this. *What is he expecting I'll say?* Maggie wondered. *Does he know the truth about the special place? Is he waiting for some kind of confession?*

"Oh?" was all Maggie said.

"It was one of my father's favorite places," Eliot added. "We used to fish together there ever since I was a kid. Sometimes we'd just go down to the dock and dangle our feet in the water. And he'd recite poetry to me. Just the two of us ever went there." He waited, watching her.

"I noticed the dock," Maggie said, finally.

"Would you like to go there?" Eliot asked, his words very deliberate. Maggie felt her head nodding a positive answer. *Just the two of us ever went there.*

"One day this week," she promised. Did he know? She still couldn't decide.

"I know you're tired," Eliot said, "but before I go, I have a surprise for you. I arranged it while you and Claire were on the veranda." He left her sitting at the bar, went to the big jukebox, slipped a quarter into it, and punched out a selection. Then, before the music started, he came back to the bar and reached out a hand for Maggie's. She gave him her hand and he pulled her off the stool and onto the dance floor.

"Eliot," she said, matter-of-factly. "It's getting late."

"One dance," he insisted. "This is my surprise, to end an evening of celebration." And then the music started, beautiful and soft, music that peeled away the years. It was 'Some Enchanted Evening,' by Ezio Pinza. Maggie felt her legs weaken but then Eliot's strong arms were around her, holding her up, holding her tight to his chest. They moved slowly around the big dance floor, and suddenly, it seemed the way it had been, when the Moon was packed with people and the jukebox was cooking, on those summer nights when Robbie's body had smelled of shaving lotion and lake water and open air. Robbie's steady, firm body pressed against hers. It had been across the crowded dance floor of the Moon that he and Maggie first locked eyes; that was why Robbie had loved the song so. And now, with the Moon nearly empty, it all came rushing back. She lifted her head and felt Eliot's lips touching hers. Soft and warm. The wind rose up outside, and Maggie heard the screen door slamming. She must remember to close the big door and lock it before she went to bed. Eliot lifted his hands from around her waist and brought them up to cup her face. He kissed her again, his hands gently cradling. Then he pulled back to look at her, smoothing strands of hair away from her face.

"From the moment I saw you," he said, "so nervous you spilled your coffee, so like a little girl, I've been wanting to hold you." Maggie moved back then, away from him. She retreated behind the bar, reached for her cognac glass, placed it in the sink.

"It's time to call it a night," she said softly. Eliot kept his eyes on her, waited. "Gil and Maudy will be here in the morning, and I'll need to be up early," Maggie added. She pretended to be busy with the cognac bottle, recapping it, putting it back in place. But Eliot paid no attention to this.

Instead, he moved behind the bar, next to her, put his hands on her arms. Maggie felt paralyzed.

"This is crazy," she said. But something kept telling her it wasn't crazy. She had wanted him, too. She had wanted to take his hand and lead him up to the small apartment.

"Maggie," he whispered. She could feel his warm hands on her arms, holding her stiffly, his breath so near to her face.

"There's something very wrong about this," she said.

"What's wrong with it?" Eliot asked. "How is it wrong? Don't tell me it's about age, because it isn't. I know how I feel." He reached out and touched her hair.

"You don't know anything about me," said Maggie. She had felt a kind of terror rising up in her, the knowledge that this was a fast-moving train, with unforgiving tracks, this moment in time with Robert's son. And yet, part of her wanted that second chance, an opportunity to start over. He was almost half her age. How did Bridgette fit into the math of Joe's life? Maggie felt the room spinning. "You don't even know me," she said again. "You don't know anything about me."

Eliot smiled, that half-smile Maggie had remembered for so many years. "You're wrong," he said. "I know a lot of things about you. I know that you signed up for German in college and hated it. I know how you're sometimes afraid of the dark, when you wake up in the middle of the night. You love Russian plays. You hate Sundays. You once dreamed of renting a little boat and traveling the canals of England. I'm *positive* that you hate opera. That wasn't just a lucky guess. And I know that you were my father's first love."

Maggie was stunned. She leaned against the bar, steadying herself, trying to think. Then, she knew. She looked at Eliot.

"You've read my letters," she said. "You've read the letters I wrote to Rob." For a moment or two he said nothing. The sounds of the wind rose up again outside. Maggie could hear squeaks and rattles in the big building. Ghostlike stirrings. She *was* afraid of the dark, when she woke suddenly, quickly from a sleep. She *did* hate Sundays, had hated them even as a child. Everyone sat around quietly on Sundays, often in clothes they weren't comfortable in. People on Sundays always seemed to be *waiting* for something that never came. He had read her letters!

"After my father died," Eliot said, finally, "my mother told me about a box he'd put away in the basement. She said it was a box of his papers from forestry school, and that he wanted me to have it. That's what he told *her.* A month after he died, I went down to the basement and found the box. Your letters were at the bottom, under his old school papers. Did he want me to find those letters, to know the truth about you? I don't know. Nobody plans to die at forty-six of a heart attack. Maybe he would have destroyed them. Maybe. I don't know the answer to that. I only know that I *did* find them." And then Maggie remembered that Eliot had just offered, minutes earlier, to take her to the special place.

"You knew about the place under the birches," Maggie whispered, "you knew all along." Eliot was still holding her arms. Now, he pulled her closer to him.

"When I drove up here last week, I wasn't just looking for a job," he said. "I wanted to see the famous Maggie Patterson. I wanted to meet the woman my father loved before he met my mother. For over five years I've wondered about you. I've read your letters again and again. You say I don't know you? I bet I know you better than anyone alive." Maggie felt flurries in her stomach. She tried to remember the letters, especially those last ones, after Dougie had died, letters in which she poured out her deepest and darkest fears, anxieties about life and death and the rigors of just being alive that she would never reveal to Joe, to anyone but Robbie. Robbie had represented that side of her, the side that explored the abyss. And now Eliot knew that side, too. Eliot *knew.* Her hands against his chest, Maggie pushed him back, away from her and against a shelf of glasses. They rattled loudly. Eliot stared at her, his black eyes trying to read her.

"Eliot," she said, "The work on the Moon is nearly finished. I think it's best that we keep a distance, at least for a while." But he didn't seem to be listening.

"The second I saw you, Maggie," he said, "I understood why Robert Flaubert couldn't pass you by. Just like I can't pass you by. It doesn't have to do with age. It has to do with poetry, and swallows that winter at the bottoms of ponds, and harvest moons rising. It has to do with hearts, and what makes them tick." But Maggie didn't want to hear this. She felt denial rising up inside her now, denial against the night, against his words. *He's read my letters. He knows my innermost thoughts. He knows everything.*

"I'm so sorry," she told Eliot. "But you *must* go." He moved away from her and stood, his back against the bar, still watching her, his face dark with emotion. She nearly reached out and touched him then, nearly. After all—and this was the truth she'd been hiding from—it had been Eliot in her silvery dreams for the past several nights, Eliot in the canoe, Eliot turning in moonlight to touch her breasts with his cool hands. It had been Eliot, not Robbie. His eyes still on her, he backed away, left her there behind the bar. As the old jukebox groaned with replacing "Some Enchanted Evening" in its inner rack, Maggie heard the pickup engine flare to life, pebbles spitting up in the driveway, and then Eliot Flaubert was just taillights swinging left at the lovely stone fence.

Red Squirrel and Tamaracks

THE BRASS RING

Margaret, are you grieving
Over Goldengrove unleaving?
Leaves, like the things of man, you
With your fresh thought care for, can you?
. . . .
It is the blight man was born for,
It is Margaret you mourn for.

—GERARD MANLEY HOPKINS,
FROM MAGGIE'S COLLEGE TEXTBOOK

During the Canadian autumn, the deciduous tamarack tree sheds its yellow needles and they drop quietly down, adding to the blanket that protects the earth from winter. Maggie stood with her coffee, on the veranda of the Harvest Moon, and traced with her eyes the outlines of tamaracks, growing in their pure stand along the curve of lake. The tamaracks were turning to gold, jutting out now among the darker greens of surrounding softwood trees. Robert Flaubert had taught her many things about the world around her. The tamarack, for instance, had been a great friend to man for a long, long time. Not only did it make a beautiful wintertime decoration, but the Indians had used the narrow roots to stitch together strips of birch bark for their canoes. *See this?* Robbie asked her once. A fierce summer rainstorm had uprooted a dying tamarack—a larch sawfly had deleaved and then killed the tree—and so Robbie knelt before the massive root system of the prostrate tree. He pointed out one particular root, bent at a right angle. *The colonists used these to join the ribs to deck timbers in their small ships,* Robbie had said. Now, more than twenty-five years later—a lifetime for Eliot—Maggie stood with her coffee and looked again at the wonder of this northern tree. At times, she had doubted she would ever see a tamarack again. She knew they grew in New England, but because their range barely dipped below the Canadian border, she had always associated them with Little Bear Lake and the Canadian woods. And now she was back, looking at them again, and they were burnishing themselves for her, turning to pure gold in the few days since she'd arrived. She was also looking toward the end of the lake, to where Eliot had said his house was sitting, keeping him warm, protecting him from winter snows and summer lightning, just as the brown Victorian on Beauchemin had kept Maggie's family warm for so many years. But she could make nothing out at the other end of the lake—so distant was it—nothing but blue skies above and blue sky reflecting in the waters below.

He had not appeared for work, but what had she expected? In the long reaches of the night before, she had lain awake and wondered if she had done the right thing. That she was captivated by him was now apparent to her. It was like losing Robbie, and then getting him back, and then giving him up again, all in one fell swoop. *He's only two months older than Lucy,* is what kept running through her mind. How could she even imagine? How had it gone this far, that she was waking at night with his name formed between tongue and teeth? Why was it that she had been standing on the veranda all morning, ever since dawn, when the great blue heron had come to fish off the end of the diving raft? Why had she been watching the tamaracks take shape in the early light and wondering if she would hear the sound of the pickup, crunching up gravel, passing through the newly restored stone wall fence and roaring into the yard of the Moon? What would the English Department say? Especially Mr. Walton, the expert in Milton, whose great passion in life was a blue and red macaw, condemned to living in a cage, who had been taught by Mr. Walton to say, "Ahhhh, Paradise Lost, Ahhh, Paradise Lost." And Sharon Lipmann, who taught Elizabethan Lyric, and played bridge every Friday night with three people from the Art Department, her greatest joy. But most importantly, Diana and Lucy: What would *they* say? Maggie knew already. "Mom, you're middle-age crazy a little late," the analytical Lucy would say. And she would be very displeased with her mother, very displeased. "Go for it, Mom," would be Diana's input. Diana, the romantic one, the family poet. "You live once, so grab the brass ring every chance you get." And that was what bothered her most, this "you live once" notion. Because it reminded her that Robert Flaubert was gone forever. He had had his moment in the sun on Little Bear Lake. So, was Maggie trying to make him live *twice*? Was she trying to make him live *again* through Eliot?

At ten o'clock Claire tromped up the stairs to Maggie's little apartment for her cup of coffee. She frowned when she picked up the glass pot and saw the molasses-like mixture clinging to the bottom. Maggie took the pot from her.

"Let me make some fresh," she offered. "This has been sitting here for a long time." She didn't want to tell Claire that she'd gotten up at dawn and made the coffee, that she and the herons and the loons had watched the mist rise on the lake together.

"I expected to be here by eight," said Claire,

fighting back a full yawn. "But I was just so beat, I fell back asleep after the alarm went off. I never thought I'd say this, but thank God for mothers who come in and make their children *rise and shine.*" Maggie forced a quick smile. She had rinsed the pot, placed a filter and coffee in the cup, and then flicked the On button. Mr. Coffee began his noisy work.

"So where is Eliot?" Claire asked. "I see that the painters are downstairs doing the dance floor. Wasn't he supposed to be here for that?" Claire flopped down into a chair at Maggie's little kitchen table and waited for the coffee. Maggie tried to decide what she should say about the incident the night before, if anything. It was true that at eight o'clock, when the painters arrived, there had been no sign of Eliot. So she had left her vigil on the screened-in veranda, where she had been sitting with her coffee, wrapped in the same sweater from the night before, sitting and watching the tamaracks, peering at Eliot's end of the lake, and wondering how it was all going to unfold. Wondering what she would say to him when he arrived. But the painters had roared into the drive in their white-panel truck with ON-THE-LAKE PAINTERS decorating the side and they had gone to work under Maggie's own instructions. It was then that she had wondered if he would come at all. And then, was it perhaps best that he didn't?

That had been at eight o'clock. Now, it was past ten, and the problem was what to tell Claire.

"He must have overslept," Maggie said as she poured Claire a fresh cup of coffee.

"I know the feeling," said Claire, taking the cup of coffee from Maggie. "I gotta pick up all those autumn decorations I ordered in Coreyville. As if we need fake colored leaves here in Little Bear. And then I got a thousand other errands. I'm outta here. Thanks for the coffee." She was gone, and no explanation was necessary. Left behind, in the still of the little upstairs kitchen, with the rhythmic sound of voices floating up from below as the painters painted, was Eliot's absence, fluttering in the air like a moth. At dawn, when Maggie had sat upon the veranda and listened to the lake come to life, she had sincerely believed that the best thing would be for him to decide not to return. It would be the *best* thing. After all, she couldn't fire him, couldn't fire Robbie's son. What would that do to him, to his already wounded self-esteem? What would that say to the town of Little Bear Lake, which would surely find out? Maggie knew that most of the people who live in little towns have eyes in the backs of their heads. So she was certain, as the sun rose over the eastern slope of mountain, that the best thing was for him to decide to stay away on his own, for him to take the initiative to do so. She was *certain*. She had said this to the great blue heron, as it fished off the diving raft. She had said it to the red squirrels, as they raced about in the tops of the branches. She had said it to the wind in the tamaracks, the sun on the lake. But now, with that same sun streaming toward noon in the sky and still no sign of the pickup, she was no longer certain of anything.

It was five o'clock when Claire returned from Coreyville, the backseat of her car loaded down with shopping bags and the trunk filled with boxes.

"It's been a long day, even if it did start at ten," Claire said. Maggie helped her carry everything into the bar. Claire stopped just long enough for a glass of water, and then she was on her way back out the front door.

"I'll see you tomorrow," she called over her shoulder. "Tell Eliot that I picked up his order of records at Radio Shack. And, oh yes, tell him that Mr. McNair said that the fixtures were in for the bathrooms." Maggie merely nodded, and soon Claire was gone again, her little Chevy Vega tearing up dust in the driveway. Maggie congratulated the painters on a job well done, wrote them out a check for their day's work, and then they, too, were gone. But there was still no sign of Eliot Flaubert.

At seven o'clock she cooked dinner for herself in the tiny kitchen, arranged her plate and wine-glass on a dinner tray, and then carried it down to the screened-in veranda. And, with the waters of Little Bear Lake lapping all around her, she managed to push her fork into a few peas, nudge the two small boiled potatoes around and around on her plate, sip a few sips of wine. And then dinner was over. Out on the lake, the loons cried out to each other. Maggie walked down to the water's edge, where she could see the little dock much better, the one that gave away the special place. A ring-billed seagull perched on one of the posts, the only visitor. No Eliot. No ghost of his father. She considered going there, through the wooded path, through the brambles and the fallen trees, into the grove of birches. "I just want to make sure that he's all right," she told herself. But she knew that this wasn't true. She wanted more than that.

Long after night had settled down upon the lake, just a few minutes past ten, the phone rang. Maggie had been reading in the little study and now she jumped, her book closing on her page, her glass of mineral water spilling itself on the coffee table.

"Hello?" she said, waiting to hear his voice. She would pretend she was merely concerned about his well-being. She would not let him know how her heart was beating at the terror of never seeing him again.

It was Lucy. "Mom? Can we talk?" And so they chatted, about her classes, about the Moon.

"Will you come for Thanksgiving then?" Maggie asked. "Since you can't make the harvest moon dance?" Lucy was noncommittal, more so than usual. She would have to see first, she said. There were classes to think about, and backpacking trips to be taken. She would try, however.

"I'll send you and Diana tickets," Maggie offered, knowing this gesture was essential, what with the girls both budgeting greatly in their lives as true adults.

"Maybe," said Lucy. Maggie thought perhaps the aftermath of divorce had caught her daughter up in its wake. Lucy was the oldest, after all, and had always seemed to shoulder the lion's share of all family burdens. Lucy was the first to feel the blow. It had always been that way, with the deaths of relatives, pets, school disappointments, canceled family vacations, world famine. You name it, Lucy's backpack carried a bit of it all. Hearing her daughter's voice, sensing an upheaval somewhere, Maggie instantly forgot about her own upheaval with Eliot. She concentrated instead on Lucy.

"Honey," she said. "Is something wrong? I'm all ears. I'm here if you want to talk." She waited. She could hear Lucy on the other end of the line, large sighs and something like a pencil beating against another object: all signs of *Lucy Distressed*. Finally Lucy decided to say what she had obviously phoned to say.

"Mom," she said, flatly. "She's pregnant."

Maggie felt a numbness in her face, her chest. Diana pregnant? Oh no, not Diana, not one of her girls, not so young, not with so much life out there to wade through first. "Can you even believe that?" Lucy asked, and now Maggie could hear the anger in her voice. Lucy wouldn't be *angry* that her sister was pregnant. She would be somewhat anguished. Yet Lucy was angry. And then Maggie knew. For the record, she asked.

"Sweetie," she said calmly, "who's pregnant?"

"Bridgette!" Lucy cried. "Who else? I'm so *embarrassed*." Maggie shook her head. She tried to put it all in perspective. Poor Lucy and Diana. This was more of that *blood of their blood* ancestor stuff. They were bound for life now to Bridgette. And this new baby, an innocent stranger. *Bone of their bone*.

"You've got nothing to be embarrassed of," Maggie assured her. "You've done nothing wrong. And this isn't as bad as it seems. Imagine having a little baby around. It'll be a whole new experience for you." She suddenly realized that Joe would be well over seventy when his and Bridgette's child was Lucy's age. *There* was a sixties bad acid trip for you.

"You mean you don't *care?*" Lucy asked. Maggie had to smile. They were still looking out for her, the girls were, still protective of her since the separation from their father.

"Not in the same way *you* care," said Maggie. "So don't feel bad for me, honey. Don't worry. It'll all be fine."

After she and Lucy had said their good-byes, Maggie hung up the phone and cried for an hour. Joe and Bridgette having a baby! Why was it bothering her so? Why didn't she expect that it was bound to happen sooner or later? Hadn't she walked away for good from the life, and the house, and the man in the brown Victorian on Beauchemin Street? Or was it jealousy? Jealousy that Joe was starting over with someone new, sans conscience bothering him, and she, Maggie Patterson, couldn't seem to do the same? Whatever it was, it hurt.

Maggie was awake when dawn made itself known outside her window. For the second day in a row, she heard the first ravens begin their quest for food. She had decided a lot of things during the course of the long night. For one, there were worse happenings than little babies being born to the world. The girls would fall in love with this half-sibling of theirs, would learn and grow. Joe would be kept young, would be kept up with the current hit songs of 2015, which would be about the year he'd be attending another high school graduation, his third. Maggie knew now that people like Joe *needed* to be kept young by *somebody, something.* So, there were worse things than babies. And she knew, as dawn blanketed Little Bear Lake and she imagined the great blue heron fishing off his raft, she knew that you can't make ghosts come to life: Robert Flaubert was among the eternally missing. She would learn to live with that. And, finally, if she could just get a good night's sleep, she would see to it that Little Bear Lake had the finest harvest moon dance, three days away, that it had ever seen at the Moon. If she could just get some sleep. And if she could just get Eliot out of her mind.

The Screech Owl

E-1 ON THE JUKEBOX

> **harvest moon:** the full moon nearest the autumnal equinox . . . because the harvest moon, like any full moon, must rise near the hour of sunset, harvest workers in the Northern Hemisphere may be aided by bright moonlight after sunset on several successive evenings . . .
>
> —FROM MAGGIE'S OLD COLLEGE DICTIONARY

At nine o'clock the next morning, a beautiful Little Bear Lake Friday morning, Maggie woke to the rattle of voices in the yard. She had been sleeping so soundly that she had not heard vehicles pull into the driveway, or doors slam, or toolboxes being hoisted about. Nothing. But she had needed the three hours of deep sleep that she was afforded. She pushed the button on the Mr. Coffee and then peered out into the yard, hoping to see Eliot's truck. She had savored the moment, had not gone straight to the kitchen window to look down. She had washed her face, brushed her teeth—no time for a shower this morning—and then come to the kitchen to make the coffee before she pulled the curtain aside to see what was what. Savoring. Her heart beginning to beat fiercely as she finally looked down into the yard. What she saw was Claire's car and another vehicle that she hadn't seen before at the Moon, a red something or other, shining from below. And then there was Gil and Maudy's older model Ford, driven up beneath the huge old maple tree in the yard, Gil's parking space for more than a quarter of a century. No truck. But especially, no truck belonging to Eliot Flaubert. Unless he had come in the red car, had borrowed it perhaps. Maggie sighed. What was happening to her? As Claire had said of Charlie, her philandering first husband, Maggie needed to get *a big dose of reality.*

From the doorway to the bar Maggie could hear Claire's voice rising nicely in the crisp morning air. She sounded rejuvenated, well-slept, busy with excitement. From out on the veranda, Maudy was instructing Gil in the art of hanging some outdoor ornament.

"It's crooked, Gilbert," she heard Maudy say. "Turn it a little to the left. That's better."

"Now look at it," Gil was saying. "Now it's *really* crooked."

Workers were noisily exchanging instructions in one of the bathrooms. Maggie could hear them well from the bar area, where she had stopped to see what Claire was doing. The big jukebox had been pulled out from its place against the wall and Claire was busy at its back. Before Maggie spoke, she listened to the voices coming from the bathroom, voices filled with talk about the fixtures that were obviously being installed. She waited to hear Eliot's voice, but there was no sound of it.

"Good morning," Maggie finally said to Claire, who peered out from behind the massive jukebox and smiled. "You're looking and sounding chipper this morning," Maggie added.

"Wish I could say the same for you," Claire noted. "You been sleeping well?"

Maggie shrugged. "All this grand opening excitement," she said. "But I still got another day to catch up. Now, whatever are you doing?" Claire came out from behind the jukebox and, with Maggie's help, shoved the huge creature back against the wall.

"Eliot's not feeling well," Claire said. "He called me last night to tell me that he was sending someone over today to take care of the bathroom fixtures." Maggie could feel her face redden just a bit, so she went behind the bar for a glass of orange juice, hoping Claire wouldn't see.

"Not feeling well?" she asked, as she leaned down into the cooler and found the bottle. Claire didn't seem to notice anything. She was now climbing a stepladder at the doorway leading onto the dance floor, her hands full of artificial colored leaves.

"He's probably just run-down, too," said Claire. "We've all put in a lot of hours the past couple weeks. Oh yes, I put those records he ordered into the jukebox for him. The ones I told you I picked up yesterday in Coreyville? The record he wanted more than anything arrived, too. The teenage clerk at Radio Shack said she didn't know they made records anymore. She kept looking at one like it was from the Stone Age. Now don't tell Eliot that I told you this, but he ordered that record for you, as a surprise. And, you'll love this. It's by Neil Young. Did you know he's Canadian?" Maggie was thankful that Claire was rattling on in her usual fashion. It meant that she wasn't aware of Maggie's discomfort.

"That's sweet," said Maggie. "And yes, I know that Neil Young is Canadian. Was it supposed to be some big secret or something?"

Maudy and Gil had obviously worked out their differences on the art of hanging things, for they appeared in the doorway in fine spirits.

"Lovely morning, ain't it?" Maudy asked. She gave Maggie a soft little hug. Gil waved at the women and then disappeared in the direction of the bathroom voices.

"He thinks he has to oversee *everything,*" Maudy whispered.

"Well, at least we're in good hands," said Maggie.

"Now Claire, sweetie," Maudy said. She had moved to the foot of the stepladder and was peering up at Claire, who was now holding fake leaves in her mouth, as she strung them along the heavy twine she had run from one corner of the room to another. "Are you sure you got enough veggies and fruit for the platters?"

"Yes, Maudy," said Claire, through the leaves in her mouth.

"And what about those little funny things that Maggie wanted?"

"The canapés," said Claire. "I got them, Maudy."

"And the cold salads from the deli?"

"Got them." Claire glared at Maggie over the top of Maudy's gray head, and raised her eyebrows into their famous arch. Maggie arched her own, as if to say, *You work it out, Claire, girl.* Then she moved away from the two women and peered through the window into the front yard. Still Claire's car, Gil's Ford under the maple, and the new red car. With Maudy behind her giving more instructions to an exasperated Claire, Maggie went out through the screen door and onto the big veranda. There beside the door was hanging the fruit of Maudy and Gil's morning activity: two lovely artificial cornucopias, spilling fake apples and grapes and acorns and autumn leaves, but lovely just the same. A true *country* touch. From the veranda, Maggie could just barely see the end of the dock, marking the special place, but no sign of life, not even the ring-billed gull that seemed to so like it as a perching place. No sign of life. Farther across the lake, boaters were specks on the water, fishermen getting in the last of the autumn fishing before the season closed. But it was too far away to see Eliot's house. She could only assume that he was there. Was he staring back at her, perhaps, from a deck? Robert would've built a deck when he built himself a house, no doubt about that. There was an unspoken law among the folks who live on lakes: You don't live on water without a deck. Was Eliot out there, watching the boaters from his side of the lake, from another perspective? Could he see the Moon from where he was, large and white and sprawling?

At noon, when the two men working in the bathroom had finished with the plumbing and with installing the new fixtures, Maggie got out her checkbook, the new one that said THE HARVEST MOON on all her checks, and readied herself to write one up. She was surprised to see how young her workers were as they approached the bar, throwing off their work gloves and reaching for the glasses of ice tea Maudy had offered them. Gil made hasty introductions.

"Friends of Eliot's," he added. Maggie merely nodded.

"A pleasure to meet you both," she said. "Now what do I owe you?" The taller of the two looked at her curiously. He shook his head.

"You don't owe us anything," he said. "Eliot called in a favor, one of the hundred we owe him."

Maggie's face obviously showed her confusion.

"Eliot is the Mr. Handyman of Little Bear Lake," said the other. "But he never charges his friends for anything. He fixed my boat for free last week, and he helped me shingle the roof on my camp last month. So he asked me to do what work was left in the bathrooms. I brought my brother along to teach him a few things about plumbing." He nodded his head at the young man with him. "No big deal," he added, and then smiled.

Maggie closed her checkbook. She was in the country, no doubt about it. "Thanks, both of you," she said, extending her hand. "If you two turn up for the dance tomorrow night, all drinks are on me."

"Even if they weren't, we'd be here," said the taller man. "We haven't danced since this place closed down."

"You *can't* dance anyway," the other said. "We

were spared the sight for three years." He smiled at Maggie.

"See you at the dance," she told him, and watched as they piled into the red car and disappeared, Gil and Maudy in the old Ford behind them. Now only Claire was left, climbing down from her ladder and surveying the canopy of leaves that grew above her head. She bobbed her chin at her work.

"Well?" she asked Maggie. "What do you think?"

Maggie looked up at the sky of fake maple leaves hanging above her head. She nodded appreciatively. "I think they look great," she said.

"Oh, I don't mean the leaves," said Claire. She turned and looked at Maggie, with her old *I can see right through you* look. "I mean, what do you think is *really* wrong with Eliot?"

Maggie and Claire sat on the veranda, sipping Irish coffees that Maggie had made up in her little kitchen, and said nothing for a long time. Maggie was the first to speak, knowing that Claire was giving her time to arrange her thoughts. It was she, Maggie, who had suggested that they sit and talk. She needed to discuss this with someone, and Claire obviously had wind that something was up.

"What am I going to do?" Maggie finally asked,

looking over at her friend, wishing she had an answer. "Do you have any idea what it feels like to wake up and discover that you're captivated with your old boyfriend's *son*?"

Claire shook her head. "This is a wild one," she said. "This one's hard to call, and I thought I could call them all."

The last piece of sun slipped behind the western side of the lake and disappeared. Maggie watched as the sky turned yellow in reflection, then crimson, then pink, in just minutes. Nature painting the sky. Nature doing a little bit of decorating on her own.

"It's about to drive me crazy, Claire," said Maggie. "I'm not sleeping at night. And now I'm worried about him. He's been through enough lately."

Claire nodded. She finished the last of her coffee and thumped the cup down on the table. She stood up, wrapping her sweater about her, stood staring at the lake. Then she turned to Maggie. "Why haven't you asked me if Robbie ever forgave you?" she suddenly wanted to know.

Maggie shrugged. "Afraid of the answer, I guess."

"Well, let me tell it to you anyway," said Claire. "Because maybe it'll do you some good. He *did* forgive you. How do I know? Because he started talking about you. Granted, we had to listen to

Gary Puckett sing 'Woman, Woman, Have You Got Cheating on Your Mind?' a million times before he was ready to let go. But he did. One night, not long after he met Julia, they came into the Moon together. Julia went to another table to talk to friends she knew from Coreyville, and that's when Robbie started reminiscing about the fun the three of us had. 'Remember the night we did this or that,' he'd say. Or, 'I wonder how Maggie is getting along?' So I said, 'I'll tell you something, Robbie. I don't know if Maggie is happy or not. I hope she is. But wherever she is, whatever she's doing, she's not forgotten us here. She's remembering us, like we're remembering her.' After that night, he just seemed to see only Julia, who was beautiful, and sweet. You need to get this all in perspective, Maggie. You and Rob were first loves, and first loves are hard to let go of sometimes. First loves are clouded in romance. But that's all it was. And then it was over."

"He forgave me?" Maggie asked softly, afraid she might cry. Claire nodded.

"I could've told you right away," Claire said, "the minute you sailed into Little Bear. I was waiting for you to ask. But, Maggie, there was really nothing to forgive. You were both so young."

"Life shouldn't be this strange," said Maggie, "at least not without an instruction booklet."

"Know what I really think about all this?" Claire finally asked. Maggie shook her head. She didn't know what *anyone* thought anymore, not Claire, not Eliot, not even herself.

"Tell me," said Maggie. "Tell me what *you* think."

Claire knelt by her chair, looked up at her face, into her eyes. Then she reached for Maggie's hand and patted it.

"I think that love in any form, in any size, in any shape, when it's *real* love, is worth it," said Claire. "Now, what you have to decide is if it's *real* love. This isn't 1969, honey. As long as you really know that, you've got nothing to worry about. What you have to decide is if you do. Now, I gotta run. How about coffee in the morning, right here, same chairs?"

Maggie nodded. "Eight o'clock?" she asked.

"It's gonna be great when the grand opening is over and we start sleeping until ten," Claire said. "My internal clock thinks I've forsaken it." Then she hugged Maggie good night, and was gone.

After dinner, on one of the tables in front of a roaring fire in the big old fireplace, Maggie felt exhausted. She sat for a long time, sipping at her glass of red wine, watching the flames dance about before her, embers flaming blue and yellow. *It isn't the firewood that burns, not directly,* Robbie had told her once, as the two of them sat before this same fireplace, listening to summer rain pelt the immense roof. *The heat drives a gas from the wood, and when that gas combines with oxygen in the air, it ignites.* He had taught her so many things, things she would never learn in all those courses she had taken in history, and art, and music, and literature. The *important* things about nature, the things you just don't find in college textbooks. *See these cattails, Maggie? If you're hungry, you'll never starve if cattails are growing nearby. You can peel the roots and cook them just like potatoes.* This had been in reference to the swampy area across from the Moon, in the huge field where the red-winged blackbirds loved to gather in clusters. They had gone there on field trips, with Robbie pointing out each bird, each flower, each butterfly, sometimes making Maggie wait while he quickly sketched them on his drawing pad. *You can even dry the roots and pound them into flour. And then the sprouts can be steamed. Have you ever heard of Russian asparagus?* Many things. What would he say about human nature now? What would he say if he knew what she was feeling about his son?

Maggie rose, glass of wine in hand, and left the blazing fire behind. She stepped out onto the veranda and stood listening to the night. She could hear the lonesome sound of a car circling the lake, following the lake road, and then she saw its headlights, two white beams of light that the car seemed to be racing to catch. Soon the white beams had transformed into red taillights, as the car raced farther from her, two red cigarette tips in the black night. And then they, too, were gone. Seconds later, even the sound of the car engine had vanished, and it seemed as if she had imagined the lonely car, circling the lake. The night grew quiet again. She heard the desolate eerie wail of a screech owl, echoing off the water in long quavery hoots. The first time she had ever heard it, at Little Bear Lake, it had frightened her, city girl that she was, and so ghostly the sound, so haunting. Robbie had laughed at her at first and then, seeing how frightened she was, said, *It's small, Maggie, just a little bird, as owls go.* Later, wanting her to forget the supernatural cry, he had turned scientific. *It's a messy eater, the screech owl. It swallows its prey whole or in chunks, and then regurgitates the fur, bones and feathers in a compact pellet.* Hearing this, she had covered her ears, remembering the plaintive cry. *Please,* she had begged him. *No more.* By summer's end, she had come to love the unearthly song of the screech owl. Even its table manners no longer upset her. Standing there on the veranda, Maggie listened again for the bird, waited to hear it, hear it and remember. But instead her ears picked up something else: music floating to her from the little dock, at the special place, music from off the night waters. Eliot. She listened for a time, trying to imagine him there in the gray of evening. For three days he had stayed away from the Moon. What was he thinking? Would he stay away forever? As Maggie stood on the veranda and listened, she could feel him out there, as though he were a part of the night, of the earth, of the waters eating up the shoreline.

Back inside the bar, Maggie opened the cash register and took out a couple of quarters. Claire had been to the bank, getting ones and fives and tens and all denominations of change. At the jukebox Maggie leaned forward, resting one arm on its face as she peered down at the selections. It wasn't difficult to tell who had chosen "Clair," by Gilbert O'Sullivan. She read on. They were all there, all of Robbie's favorite songs when they had first met, old songs, classic songs. "Blue Moon" (Boy Wants Girl). "Some Enchanted Evening" (Boy Meets Girl). "Stranger in Paradise" (Boy Falls In Love With Girl). "You Send Me" (It Gets Serious). "Light My Fire" (Real Serious).

Music never goes away, Maggie thought. Like light, it curves somewhere in space and comes back, bringing with it all the same emotion, all the same laughter, all the same pain. She read the titles again. Sam Cooke. *You send me*. He had been shot and killed in 1964, at the age of twenty-nine, probably by a white woman's jealous husband. Such a talent, such a handsome young man. Gone. Disappeared, except for the records left behind. And Ezio Pinza. Maggie pushed the buttons, M-7—M for Maggie—and soon the big booming voice filled the bar, harmonized with the orange shadows of fire that were playing on the wall, reflections from the blazing fireplace. Maggie danced, all by herself, the way Robbie used to dance to that same song, sweeping arcs, her arms held up before her as though she were waltzing with a ghost, one cradling an invisible neck, the other holding an invisible hand. Around and around the room, dancing with a memory. Or was she? When the song finished, she forced herself to return to the jukebox and peer again at the selections. There it was. Neil Young. Good old Neil, still singing, still hanging in there, still feeling the pain, still telling about it, still reeling in the good times. "Harvest Moon." That was the title of the song, written on the temporary label with Claire's neat, steady hand. No wonder Eliot had wanted to surprise her. "Harvest Moon." What a perfect title for the grand opening. She pushed the letters, E-1—E for Eliot, just as Gil liked to do for his customers in the old days, his personalized alphabet. So Claire had done the same. Claire had forgotten nothing about the good ole days, or the good ole ways. The song started, slow and sweet. *Come a little bit closer, Hear what I have to say, Just like children sleepin', We could dream this night away.* Again Maggie danced, with tears in her eyes as she heard the words for the first time. She danced to the firelight. She danced to honor the loons and the lake waters, the way the Indians had danced on those same shores, around fire made from lightning and pine. She danced to honor the dead. She danced for the living. *But there's a full moon risin', Let's go dancing in the light, We know where the music's playin', Let's go out and feel the night, Because I'm still in love with you, I want to see you dance again, Because I'm still in love with you, On this harvest moon.*

Maggie's Window

THE DANCE

When we were strangers
I watched you from afar
When we were lovers
I loved you with all my heart
But now it's gettin' late
And the moon is climbin' high
I want to celebrate
See it shinin' in your eye
Because I'm still in love with you
I want to see you dance again
Because I'm still in love with you
On this harvest moon.
—"Harvest Moon," by Neil Young.

The grand opening arrived, bringing the bluest skies Maggie could ever remember at Little Bear Lake. Even Maudy felt the urge to honor the propitious event by phoning Maggie at 9:00 A.M. and asking if she'd been outside yet to take note of the cloudless sky, the blue of it reflecting nicely upon the lake, the rug of red and orange and yellow trees that had spread itself over the slopes of the hills.

"It's a made-to-order morning," Maudy told her. "I don't remember a prettier harvest moon day than this. Except that one time, remember, when it was so warm and pretty we moved the band out onto the veranda and let everyone dance by the lake. Remember? Robbie made a huge bonfire?" Maggie smiled. She remembered. And it was good to hear folks willing to speak Robert Flaubert's name in front of her. He had made a bonfire, indeed, all the while singing "Light My Fire," one of his favorite jukebox songs, entertaining everyone in the process. Robbie, circling the fire like some kind of pagan dancer.

"We'll be there early today," Maudy said. "Oh, yes, tell Eliot to make sure someone mows the hay down in that area along the stone fence. Gil says we'll need extra parking space."

"I'll tell him," said Maggie.

"I'm sure he won't forget," said Maudy. "Gil mentioned it last week. But just in case."

"Just in case," Maggie repeated. They hadn't noticed his disappearance for the past four days, so busy had everyone been, coming and going with their individual errands. But what if he didn't show up today? What if he didn't come to the dance? What would she say then by way of explanation?

Claire pulled into the driveway, raising up the dust that always seemed to trail her little Chevy Vega. Maggie was standing at the door to the bar when Claire came in, two sacks in her arms.

"Good morning, Mrs. Robinson," she said to Maggie, but Maggie said nothing. She couldn't even smile at this, although she knew that humor was always Claire's remedy for a tense moment. Maggie watched as Claire deposited the sacks upon the bar.

"Well?" she finally asked.

"I've left four messages since last night," Claire said. "He hasn't returned a single call. So I drove past the house this morning, on my way here. No sign of his truck. What can I tell you?"

Maggie said nothing. Instead she left Claire behind the bar, working furiously on the schedules for the four waitresses she had hired. All four were to work that night, considering how busy the Moon should be. Then Claire would juggle schedules for those less busy nights and weekends until summer brought its onslaught of tourists. "The Hargrove girl is about as graceful as you used to be," Claire had told Maggie a week earlier. Now, it all seemed so unimportant. What had once been Maggie's Magnificent Adventure was turning sour and now Maggie was wondering why. Why was this young man filling up her thoughts so that everything else in her life was sinking into second place? Eliot Flaubert. Robert's son. She wondered what her mother would say if she could speak to Maggie just then, from whatever dimension she was residing in. She was missing her mother more and more these days, wishing her mother could see her now, with a business to run, without a husband, without even her children. Would Diana Patterson be proud of her daughter, or disappointed? Owning the Moon was a solo venture that Maggie's mother could never have envisioned for herself. Maggie's mother had been the proper New England housewife, dinner on the table at the same time every night, always politely deferring to her husband in times of decision making. Maggie remembered the white gloves she and her mother wore to church every Sunday, until Maggie reached her freshman year in high school and began the rebellious period of her life. But how could she not rebel? The sixties were uncurling all around her, rapid as a grass fire, with women burning their bras and demanding their equal share of the American pie. And, being a child of those groundbreaking years, Maggie had vowed her own daughters would never wear white gloves on Sundays, or on any other day. Funny, but it would have been easier to envision a tryst with Eliot back in the late sixties, in that time when she first met his father. But something had happened over the years, something had changed in most baby-boomer flower children after they'd raised their own families: An aura of conservatism was creeping back. And so was Maggie's New England upbringing. At the age of forty-six, she was wondering for the first time in her life what her mother would think about her choice in men!

Maggie heard a buzzing start up out near the road. She and Claire moved to the window. Up at the stone wall fence was another young man, a gas-powered weed eater attached to his body with a huge strap. He was cutting down the hay to make way for more parking.

"Steve O'Neal," said Claire, taking note. "Another of Eliot's friends." Maggie watched as row after row of hay and weeds and dying grass fell before the weed eater.

"I guess Steve owes Eliot a favor, too," Maggie said, finally.

Claire nodded. "Looks like it," she said.

Maggie walked down to the water's edge and stood looking out across the expanse as though it were spread before her like a future that might be, if you could *see* the future, just a wide blue blanket, unspoiled yet, untrodden, waiting for someone to make a mark on it.

"You okay, sweetie?" Claire called from the porch. "Your footprints are gonna end up permanent down there. Archaeologists, thousands of years from now, will think some great ritual was carried out there by the water." Maggie looked down the stretch of shoreline and water, to where the little dock, empty except for its loyal ring-billed gull, pushed out into the water.

"I'm okay," she finally answered Claire. "But I think this *is* some kind of ritual." And then she turned back to the Moon, back to the impossibly busy day and evening which lay ahead: the harvest moon dance.

They came in small groups, singles, and eight at a time, but they came, folks from Little Bear Lake, from Coreyville, from Percyton, from all the surrounding small towns and big towns. They came to the harvest moon dance. In 1958, when Gil and Maudy had first opened the Moon, they had set the tradition of dress for the dance: suit and tie for the men, the prettiest dresses the girls and women could find in the local stores. "There aren't a lot of occasions to dress up, here in Little Bear Lake," Maudy had told Maggie during her first harvest moon dance, in 1967, when she had taken a long weekend from her studies at Boston University in order to drive up for the occasion. It was the handsome Robert Flaubert who had provided the lure, however, not the opportunity to wear a new dress to yet another dance. Robbie Flaubert always turned up in jeans anyway, a gesture not of rudeness but of his own sense of himself. No one had seemed to mind, except Maudy. But Maggie realized that very first September that the dance was special to Robbie, and to the locals, perhaps as a last chance to celebrate the end of summer, to prepare for the long cold winter that lay ahead. The way their Celtic ancestors had placed green boughs about their houses during the winter solstice, green to remember summer, green that would eventually turn into the green now used to decorate at Christmas. The dance was a *ritual*, and now, since it had begun in 1958, there were many locals who had been *born* to the tradition. It was another Christmas to them. Another Thanksgiving. Another excuse to gather together as a community and exchange pleasantries, release tensions, reexamine the very course of their lives. A ritual. Would Eliot break a ritual he'd been born into?

The hors d'oeuvres were a big hit, as were the autumny decorations Claire had spread throughout the bar and along the sides of the dance floor. A small log was all Maggie dared to ignite in the massive fireplace, so warm was the evening of the harvest moon, September 23, 1995. Only to please Maudy, she had decided to wear a dress for the event, although it was obvious that things had changed in the twenty-five years she'd been away. Some of the young girls were turning up in pants, a couple wearing jeans. Maudy was a bit perturbed. "It's all so different these days," she'd whispered to Maggie. But Maggie and Claire had been children of the sixties, children of that decade they couldn't seem to outrun. At least according to Claire. Comfort was still the operative word. "I'll be damned if I'm going to work behind that bar dressed as one of the Gabor sisters just to please Maudy," Claire had said, as she turned up in her customary jeans and baggy cotton shirt. "Just let her say something to me." Maggie had caught Maudy's reaction, a *tsk-tsk* look on her face, when she first saw Claire's outfit. A quick shake of her head, as if to dispel her negative thoughts. And that was it.

The band from Coreyville was good, especially by "local band" standards, and soon the Harvest Moon was rocking with the sound of foot-beats on the big square dance floor. Gil and Maudy were in their element again, passing out plates of canapés and seeing that everyone was comfortable. Claire looked frazzled but pleased behind the bar as she and the part-time bartender she had hired poured drink after drink for the waitresses, who kept bustling back and forth with their trays. Just that morning Claire had asked Maggie to consider the possibility of the two of them becoming business partners. "I couldn't afford to buy this place on my own," Claire had said, "which is what

I wanted to do when I moved back here and saw what a good business prospect it was. But I could swing half, in a few months." Maggie liked the idea, the notion of sharing the responsibility. And it looked like it *was* going to be a good business venture, after all. So much for Joe McIntyre and his prophecy of doom. Joe would need to content himself with picking out cribs and stockpiling diapers. Maggie would run the Harvest Moon.

At ten o'clock Eliot still hadn't shown up. The band had taken their second break of the evening, and the young local girls seemed to like the new songs Eliot had chosen for the jukebox. They filled it with quarters at each break. Maggie kept scanning the crowd, as the evening wore on, hoping to catch those black eyes just above the line of dancers.

"Have you seen him?" she leaned over the bar once to ask Claire, who shook her head and went back to mixing Bloody Marys. Strangely, Gil and Maudy were so busy introducing Maggie to her fellow Little Bear Lakers that they didn't seem to notice that Eliot was missing. Some of the locals remembered Maggie from years ago, others were too young. But they welcomed her with open arms. "So good to see the Moon up and running again," they told her. "Welcome to Little Bear Lake. Welcome to our community." She would have been floating on air if Eliot had been there.

She wasn't sure what she would do if and when he did turn up. But she was worried about him, worried about his state of mind.

At a quarter to eleven, Maggie thought her insides would simply chew her up, so tense were the muscles in her stomach. *He isn't coming. He isn't coming to the ritual.* Having started at eight o'clock, the band was on their third break of the night. They would play, for this special dance, from eight until a quarter to one. In the future, all bands would begin at 9 P.M. Maudy was introducing Maggie to the local librarian, Peggy Montgomery, knowing Maggie would be most happy to discuss books with her, and to inquire about upcoming library events. And it was in the middle of this conversation about how the library hoped to lure well-known writers to that part of the country to read from their works, that Maggie heard the song, the one by Neil Young, Eliot's song. No one had played it all night, till now, perhaps because it was already a few years old, and the young tire quickly of things. But there it was. *Come a little bit closer, Hear what I have to say, Just like children sleepin', We could dream this night away.* And it seemed as if the roar of the crowd dropped for her to hear the words, winging like birds about the big dance floor. She looked immediately, instinctively toward the bar, because this is where Robbie had sat, all those nights he waited for her to finish with her waitressing. And there he was. There sat Eliot, his black eyes watching her intently, his face the only thing she could see in that immense room of people, people eating, people talking, people drinking, people dancing to the song, people laughing. THE HARVEST MOON: DANCING & COCKTAILS. She saw Eliot's face. *But now it's gettin' late, And the moon is climbin' high, I want to celebrate, See it shinin' in your eye, On this harvest moon.* And then a large group of people moved between them and his face was gone, lost in the sea of faces that had washed it away. Eliot.

Saying good-bye to Peggy Montgomery, Maggie made her way to the bar. By the time she got there, Eliot was nowhere to be seen. Claire motioned for her to lean over the bar. She had something to whisper to her.

"I think you could end up in the *Guinness Book of World Records* for this," Claire whispered. Maggie knotted her eyebrows.

"Why?" she asked.

"Breaking two generations of hearts," Claire answered. "I don't think anyone has laid claim to *that* record yet. Not even Cher." Maggie couldn't smile. She took the glass of wine Claire offered her. She had been sipping on one earlier and then put it down only to forget where. There had been so many people to meet, so many hands to shake, so many faces to attach names to. Gil and

Maudy had been dragging her by the elbow all night, introducing her to this one and that one. Now they seemed finished with her, content to enjoy the rest of the dance from the chairs on the veranda, where it was cooler and the band not so loud.

"Where is he?" Maggie asked, but Claire simply shrugged.

"I thought you hired me to sling drinks," she said to Maggie. "Want me to stop and look for Eliot? Keep this in mind. Wherever he is, he's in love. That's pretty obvious." Maggie frowned at her. People pushed into the bar area. They seemed to be coming from every corner, every nook, every cranny. Was there anyone left in Little Bear Lake, in Coreyville, in Lakeview? The Harvest Moon was groaning with the weight and pressure of bodies. Maggie imagined that the surrounding towns might look as though the Pied Piper had just swept through there. And then the next song caught her attention, Ezio Pinza's big booming voice, a thundering voice, the old jukebox reverberating with it. Robbie's old song, now being played by Eliot. She had no doubt that it was Eliot. No doubt. "Some Enchanted Evening."

And there he was, staring at her from the opposite side of the room again, where she had just been standing, talking to Peggy Montgomery. Was he playing games with her? Was he trying to be elusive, or had he gone over there to find her? Maggie smiled, but Eliot didn't smile back. She could see he was wearing a red T-shirt, red that brought out his black eyes and crow-black hair, and he was wearing jeans. Wait until Maudy caught him. She was forever pleading with Robbie to wear a suit.

Eliot never took his eyes from her as the song played. What was she going to say to him? "Eliot, let's be friends. This other thing is too big for us to handle. Are you okay? Let's be friends." It was so good to finally see him again. She tried to ask herself why her stomach was turning over, the way it does when you first fall in love, a stomach full of fluttering butterflies. Tension, that's what it was, tension over the grand opening, and then worrying about Eliot. His hair was so dark against that red T-shirt. He had now leaned back against the wall, his arms folded, still watching her. She had been trying to make her way to him, through the crowd of people, people stopping her to congratulate her on the grand opening, people who had already congratulated her but who felt the merry need to congratulate her yet again. When she got to the other side of the room, the song was over. The band was now back playing, and more people than ever rushed the dance floor. But Eliot was gone.

"Have you seen Eliot?" Maggie asked Gil. He

had come in from off the veranda for another glass of scotch, Maudy having agreed earlier that this was a night Gil could kick up his heels and have three scotches, just as he had done in the old days.

"He just got in his truck and drove away," said Gil. "I tried to holler out to him, ask him why he was leaving, but he didn't hear me. Now, my girl, how's it feel to be a club owner on a full night? Good, huh? Well, I'll be back for a Saturday night in January, when it's twenty-five below zero, and we'll talk." He winked. Maggie felt suddenly that the night was over, the magical night had lost its touch, what with Eliot gone.

She spent the rest of the evening conscious that a smile was appearing on her face. What was it T. S. Eliot had said? *There will be time, there will be time, to prepare a face to meet the faces that you meet.* Claire seemed to be all genuine smiles behind the bar.

"Don't look now, but see the good-looking guy sitting at the end of the bar?" Claire wanted to know. "He's Penny Hargrove's uncle. I know now why I hired her. She might be clumsy, but she's got good-looking relatives. This one happens to be a lawyer." Maggie glanced in that direction. *"Don't look!"* Claire whispered. "Okay, now look." Maggie saw that there was, indeed, an attractive man sitting on the last bar stool, sipping on a cocktail. "He's asked me to go to Coreyville with him for breakfast," said Claire. "The diner there stays open for breakfast until 2 A.M. on Saturday nights. I told him yes. He's waiting for me to finish." Maggie smiled and squeezed Claire's hand.

"Go now," she said. "The girls and I will clean up."

At first, Claire refused. "He said he'd wait," she whispered. But Maggie would hear nothing of it.

"Go," she said. "I'll finish up for you. You've worked hard enough these past three weeks. And he *is* attractive. You were predicting just this morning, remember, that you'd never meet anyone interesting again. Go." So Claire dried her hands on the bar towel and left with the lawyer from Coreyville, who seemed to have eyes for only her. Last call had been a quarter to one, and now it was almost one-thirty. The band was packing up. The crowd had already begun leaving as they had come, singly, as doubles, and in large groups. Gil and Maudy, rarely up so late, bid Maggie good-bye.

"Seems so funny for the bar to close and us not to go up the stairs to bed," Maudy said. "But I do love our little house in town." The clamor of automobile engines roaring to life rose up in the driveway. People said good night, looked for lost purses, made one last trip to the bathrooms. Voices filled the driveway, excited voices, the sound of life busily going on. It had been a successful dance, at least as far as the locals were concerned.

As the noise had come, it receded, like a giant wave. Left, finally, was Maggie and two of the four waitresses, tending to the aftermath, mopping floors, wiping down the bar, washing glasses, draining the beer taps. Maggie would worry about restocking the bar the next day. Besides, they weren't open again until Tuesday. Plenty of time. Finally, Maggie was left in the bar alone. Her cotton dress had become soaked with all the dishwashing, so she had gone up to change into shorts and a T-shirt. The bottoms of her feet ached. So she put them up on another bar stool and sat there, surveying the huge building.

At first, she was stunned by the silence. Had she dreamed the grand opening? Had she imagined all those people with the smiling faces and the dance steps and the toasts raised to the Moon? Had she imagined Eliot, brooding from across the room? Eliot, standing out in his red T-shirt as though it were some kind of flag. A flag of warning? "Why didn't he say hello?" she had asked Claire, who raised her famous eyebrows at the notion. "You told him to stay away," Claire reminded her. "You must remember how proud Robbie was. I'm sure Eliot is the same. I'm surprised he came at all." Silence. A whole dance hall full of it. What a loud thing it seemed, as Maggie sat at the bar. The noise of her wineglass upon the polished wood echoed throughout the building. The steady *drip drip drip* of water into the bar sink. The lapping sound of the lake through the screen door. Creaks in the house. It was enough to drive Maggie insane. There had been a Cinderella ball, and now she was alone, digging through the ashes.

Out on the veranda, she noticed the moon first, a huge orange harvest moon that had spent its evening crossing the sky over Little Bear Lake. Now it hovered there, bringing word of the harvest with it. She saw the full harvest moon, and then she heard his music, rising up from the special place. He was at the dock. He was at the special place, where Robbie used to wait for her. At first she felt indignant. Why hadn't he at least come over to say hello? After all, he had worked hard, too, and the success of the dance was partly his. Was he playing some kind of schoolboy game of being hard to get? Foolish, that's what it was. Childish. She wouldn't play that game. Another glass of wine, to help her unwind, to slow the flood of adrenaline, and she'd be fine. She'd be fine, and ready, finally, for a good long night's sleep.

She simply left an opened bottle of Louis Jadot on the bar. This was indeed a time of celebration, and of quiet reflection. The dance had been even more successful than in Gil and Maudy's day.

Maggie would celebrate alone. She would celebrate with music. She would even celebrate the impending birth of Joe's future child. Quarters: She found them in a jar Claire had left beneath the bar. All other money had been sacked up and stored in the big old safe that Gil had included in the deal as bar equipment. With a bottle of wine at the ready, with the old dance hall settling down on its haunches after such a long busy night, Maggie sipped wine, and played each of Robbie's favorite records, over and over again. "You Send Me." "Stranger in Paradise." "Blue Moon." "Light My Fire."

She went out on the veranda again, her glass in hand, and stood watching as dawn began to blotch the top of the horizon. It was after 4 A.M. The morning birds were already beginning to stir in the semidarkness. The light in the bar was still on, still spilling yellow out of the windows, attracting the late-season moths, tiny things that pitter-pattered against the window. Then, her breath caught in her throat, she listened. There it was. Soft and wavy, almost watery as it floated over the sheet of the lake: Eliot's music. Maggie listened, watched the area of cove where she knew the little dock was jutting out into the water. He would know she was still up, would know by the lights. She went back inside. Another glass of wine, another song, and then she'd be off to bed. Enough was enough. This was the emotional roller coaster of college girls and she wanted no part of it. Another glass of Louis Jadot. The song might as well be Eliot's, E-1 on the jukebox. "Harvest Moon." And so she played it. The words bounced around the large empty room, ghostly now, only the echo of laughter left behind. *Come a little bit closer, Hear what I have to say, Just like children sleepin', We can dream this night away.* Suddenly, Maggie was filled with an unimaginable longing. This was the sound of the sixties, still, of the seventies, the eternal sound of a generation. This could've been "Harvest." It could've been "Heart of Gold." It was one of the voices of her generation, still singing, still speaking, now to a younger generation.

She was filled with yearning and yet with renewal, with a sense of loss, with a sense of gain. Life and death were mingling. Robbie and Eliot. The past stopped where the future began. Robbie had told her once, "It's Mr. Einstein's theory that the past exists. We just can't see it." Well, that was interesting enough, but Maggie now understood that the future truly *did* exist, and not just in theory. We can't see it because it hasn't happened yet. It's simply waiting. Whether you believe it can be shaped or molded, or if it's already complete and waiting to happen, it nevertheless exists. *When we were strangers, I watched you from afar,*

When we were lovers, I loved you with all my heart. She left her glass of wine on the bar. Outside the tiny bar window, she could see fingers of daylight tracing the sky. She wouldn't need a flashlight. Her feet still knew the path. She had envisioned it many times, had walked it at night, during her dreams. She wouldn't need a flashlight, but she needed to tell herself the truth. She had wanted him to come to the dance, she had wanted him to ask her to dance, she had wanted him to hold her, she had wanted him to kiss her again, she had wanted him. *But now it's gettin' late, And the moon is climbin' high, I want to celebrate, See it shinin' in your eye.*

The grass was wet beneath her bare feet, soaking her cloth shoes. Her shorts and T-shirt brushed against the leaves of the trees, caught up dewdrops from the branches. Up through the brambles she went, past the chokecherry bushes and the fallen tree she had scouted earlier in the week, then up the little hill that would lead her down to the soft carpet beneath those heavenly birches. It was at the crest of this hill that she could hear the music best. What was he playing? What was Eliot playing? Was it Neil Young again? She couldn't understand the words: Although they were floating up the hill to greet her, they were meaningless. Language was insignificant, hollow, pointless. Instead, she heard wing-beats of memory again, fluttering near her ears. Yet she knew, knew in the deepest realm of her heart, that it was not Robbie. It was Eliot. And then she was descending the hill, where the path was easy, well-trodden, pushing past the sumac and into the grove of white birches. He was sitting outside the truck, on the grass that grew down to the water's edge. In the light of dawn she could see his face, his eyes unblinking as he watched her approach him. She said nothing, trying to catch her breath, trying to stop her heart from beating so wildly. He kept his eyes on her face, looking for some kind of answer. Finally he spoke, his words rising up to her, floating up where she could hear them, soft and breakable.

"Do you remember how Jay Gatsby stood on the end of his dock?" he asked, his voice like a song itself, a voice filled with sorrow. She knelt beside him on the wet grass, reached out to touch his face. His hair was damp with the dew that had settled down on the land, and so she pushed it back from his face, the feel of it in her hands like strands of silk.

"Yes," she said. "I remember." From across the lake one of the loons sang out. In the first rays of the morning, in the encroaching light, she could see Eliot's face clearly. Now his black eyes were peering straight ahead at the lights of the Harvest Moon.

"Do you remember how Jay Gatsby looked for Daisy's light across the water?" he asked her, his voice ragged. She leaned forward to kiss his face, which tasted wet to her lips, salty almost. Had he been crying? She tried to kiss him again, but he grabbed her by both arms and held her away from him so that he could look at her. "Do you *remember?*" he asked her again, his hands binding her arms, preventing her from putting them around him. She felt her body trying to slip away, to float off somewhere over the lake, to some distant spot where she could look down and see them both there on the shore.

"Yes," she cried. "I *remember.*" Then Eliot released one of her arms and she felt his hand on her breast, felt the nipple stiffen instantly beneath her T-shirt. A shiver ran over her, followed by goose bumps. He pushed her over, onto her back in the grass, lowered himself on top of her.

"I never knew till now how broken his heart was," he whispered, lifting her T-shirt up to expose her breasts. "I never knew," he said. And then he lowered his mouth to her breast. Maggie closed her eyes. She heard him unzip his jeans and pull them off. Then she moved her hips for him as he pulled her shorts down and off the ends of her feet. He drew both of her legs upward and wrapped them around his waist. She felt him against her, felt him push inside her. And then

Maggie was floating, somewhere out over the lake where the mist was lifting, where the loons themselves were floating, their red eyes open to the morning.

On the Lake

THE MORNING AFTER

Maggie woke the next morning to guilt, as though it were a rainstorm, or a flock of birds passing over in their migration. She pulled herself up in a sitting position in her bed and contemplated her fate. Did her New England ancestors ever hang women such as she? Was there a fate worse than death for her in such places as Iran and Iraq? Asleep in the bed beside her lay Eliot Flaubert. Maggie listened for a time to his breathing, watched him twitch in his sleep, the perfect outline of his nose and lips and chin. Eliot. He had driven her back in the gray light of morning, with all the birds alive around them, with the world coming to life, with yellow lights beginning to blink on around the lake. Early risers. He had driven her home as though they had been on a date, and she had let him follow her up the narrow staircase to her little apartment. Then, with the magic of the night still at work, it seemed exactly as it should have been. They had united themselves against the world and now they were lying safe in each other's arms. As it should be. But there is something about the magic of night that washes away with the light of day. Whether right or wrong, the magic diminishes, wanes, tapers off. Sometimes it's impossible to get it back.

Now Maggie had to wonder about what had caused that magic in the first place. Was Eliot the only way she could get close to Robbie, the only avenue left open that could bring her nearer to him? And, if so, was it an avenue she should have taken? And what about Eliot? Did Maggie represent his father's past, someone his father loved that he, too, could love? Was Eliot looking for that same avenue back to Robbie? As he slept beside her, she could still feel him between her thighs, the soreness of her muscles where her legs had arched themselves to hold him. She could smell the musty perfume of sex, she could *feel* him, still, could feel his lips on her breasts, the burning on her back where she had been pressed backward into the earth. Maybe at first Eliot had represented the only way she could find Robbie again, maybe that was it at first, but in doing so, she had fallen in love with him. She knew this as she watched him, a little twitch playing around his mouth, his eyes wavering with sleep. He was Robbie, and yet he was more than Robbie. She could appreciate him in ways she could never appreciate Robbie, because she hadn't been wise enough, hadn't been laden enough with life to understand the wonder of it all. She had been given a second chance, pure and simple. But could she take it? She told herself that this wasn't what Joe was doing with Bridgette. She hadn't come looking for Eliot while a family waited at home, in the lovely brown Victorian house on Beauchemin Street. She hadn't walked away from twenty-five years of marriage to take up with a younger man because she looked into the mirror one day and saw crow's feet kicking out about her eyes. Was she being fair to Joe? Was it youth he saw in Bridgette? Just pure lust? Or had he watched her day after day before he touched her, the way Maggie had done with Eliot? Had he seen in Bridgette something so precious he was willing to give up everything he once believed in, in order to just pursue it?

"I doubt it," Maggie whispered aloud, as Eliot slept. "I suspect it was lust." Eliot turned in his sleep, brought his arm up to reach out for her, and, finding her there, fell back into sleep. She wanted to say things to him, but now she knew she couldn't. The light was destroying the magic. The light was rushing in with some awful truths. What would the girls say? Lucy would predict that Maggie was just reacting to the news of Bridgette's pregnancy, and that might even be partly true. But maybe that news had edged her toward what she'd wanted to do all along: get close to Eliot, touch Eliot, love Eliot. And Diana? "Go for it, no matter what pushed you there, Mom. Grab that brass ring."

Maggie lay in bed, knowing that it must be past ten o'clock, knowing it was a Sunday after the harvest moon dance, after a rigorous three weeks of hard work. No one would be stirring early. Late in the afternoon she would hear from Claire, who would then tell her that the lawyer from Coreyville was either the next Mr. Right or a walking dud. Maybe Gil and Maudy would call to comment again on how magnificent a thing it was to see the Moon in such good hands. Before he had fallen asleep, Eliot had told her, "We're going on a picnic tomorrow, just the two of us, no Claire. We'll sit beneath the birches by the dock. I'm going to spread a tablecloth on the grass. We're having a picnic tomorrow." With his head resting against her stomach, Maggie rubbed his temples gently, lightly, so as not to wake him. He needed his sleep. She wondered now if he'd slept at all in the past four days or, like her, had been running on pure adrenaline. She ran a finger along the taut muscles of his arm. She wanted to say things to him. She wanted to say, "Listen, Eliot, I've fallen in love with you, you who are only two months older than my oldest child, Lucy, who will spend years trying hard to dislike you. There's no doubt that I love you, but consider this: It was your father, Robert Flaubert, that I first loved in you, that brought me to you. If he hadn't been there, you'd have been just a wonderful person that I might've met and enjoyed and passed by."

This is what she wanted to say, now that daylight had come and the Cinderella dance was over. But she didn't. Instead, she left him sleeping in the antique bed she had found in a dusty little shop in Coreyville. She slipped into a pair of jeans and a sweater. In the kitchen she made coffee only, her stomach too queasy to eat. She took her coffee down to the wide veranda, where the great blue heron was still fishing off the raft, and she sat in the rocker there, legs crossed. She sat and thought about Eliot Flaubert and what she would do with him. They had come back to the Moon in the light of morning. They had climbed the narrow stairway to her tiny apartment. They had made love again, this time slowly, gently, as though their bodies might break otherwise. "Nothing can grow from this," she had told him when it was over. "Nothing." And then, like a naive high school girl, crazy in love, she had cried. Eliot had held her, tried to comfort her. "Listen," he said. "This isn't about age. This is about love. This is about respect. I'm not Robert Flaubert, and I know that you know that. I'm his son. That's all, and it's enough." And then he put his head upon her chest and, with the wind playing tricks with the curtains, with the lake beginning to lap against the shoreline outside, he fell asleep in her bed. "Eliot," she had said, wanting to utter his name one more time, wanting him to know that she knew it wasn't Robert in the room. It was he. It was Eliot. "Eliot," she said, as the soft sounds of his breathing filled the tiny room. "Eliot."

Now, on the widening veranda, with a strong coffee in hand, her second thoughts had turned into fourth thoughts. Tenth thoughts. How could this work? Would she lose Lucy for a time, until she could coax her back? What about Eliot's mother? What about the residents of Little Bear Lake? What would they think? Claire had told her that times had changed. "There are several couples around here now just like you," she'd told Maggie. "You know, older woman, younger man." It sounded like some dreaded disease. But Maggie knew in her heart that it shouldn't matter if there were any other couples around or not. It wasn't about statistics. Or about feminism, or groups demanding rights. It was about *love.* It was about her and Eliot, fighting their way in the world. And above that, beyond that, he was the son of the first man she had ever loved, probably the *only* man she had ever loved, until now. Until Eliot. Was this a love that was possible? She knew *why* she loved Eliot, could answer that one instantly. It was the same attraction that had drawn her to Robbie: his knowledge of the world, of the things that you can't learn from a book. It was what Eliot said that day he had taken her to look at the stone fence. *Did you know,* he had asked, *that in the eighteenth century, people thought that swallows spent the winters at the bottom of ponds?* This was what captivated her.

As much as she had tried to avoid him, his presence had filtered its way into her mind, had established itself in her psyche. Sometimes she had heard him telling Claire about the plants he'd found growing in the field across the road from the Moon, the same field where Maggie had learned about plants from Robbie. He'd obviously been an excellent teacher to his son as well. In the two and a half weeks that Eliot had worked at the Moon, Maggie heard him tell Claire about northern shrikes depositing grasshoppers upon barbed wire spikes. He had pointed out sun dogs to Maudy, positioned on each flank of the sun, ice crystals in the upper atmosphere. *Colder weather is coming,* he had said. He had shown Gil the husks of hazelnuts chewed by dormice, pinecones gnawed on by squirrels. The night he and Maggie and Claire had stood by the edge of the lake, he had named all the major stars in Orion. *No other constellation has so many bright stars,* he had told them. This was what he knew about the earth, and Maggie saw it as so much more important and meaningful than bridge on Friday nights, or papers on Milton, or lectures on Dryden, Swift and Pope. So much more. And then he could turn to her in the dawn of a cool lake morning, he could turn and ask, *Did you know how much Jay Gatsby hurt, when he stared across the water at Daisy's little light?* This was why she had come to love him, would hate to lose him. But the math kept coming back at her, time and again, the way it must never have bothered Joe. Or did it at first? Of course, it must have. He would've wondered what Lucy would say. And Diana would never tell him to go for the brass ring when it meant leaving her mother. No, Joe must've pondered these issues greatly. His relationship was still touch and go with both of his daughters. But he had had the courage of his convictions—or his pure lust—to make the transition. Maggie realized that this was something *she* didn't have, as she sat on her morning porch, sipping her coffee, and waiting for Eliot Flaubert to wake up so that she could tell him. *We cannot do this, Eliot. Too many people will be in upheaval over our falling in love. My daughter. Your mother. Think of all the stares we'll get in restaurants. On the street. Are we prepared to pay that price? We cannot do this, Eliot.*

When she heard sounds of him stirring up in the apartment, sounds of him in the shower, Maggie phoned Claire. "Can you run the Harvest Moon by yourself?" she asked. "With me as an absentee partner?" Claire, as would be expected, was startled. "What the hell are you talking about?" she asked. "Don't you move, I'll be right there." And then Eliot came down the stairs, looking exuberant, as if the world were a thing to be taken on.

"Good morning, beautiful," he said, leaning down to kiss her, and then to tousle her hair. Had Joe ever done that? "I'll be back in less than an hour with that picnic I promised you," he said. "Are you as hungry as I am?" And so she told him, everything she had been thinking, about how their lives together would have to be lived in a fishbowl, with various people peering in at them to comment, people who were attached to their lives, strangers who had nothing to do with their lives. *We cannot do this, Eliot. We cannot.*

"I'm leaving Little Bear Lake," she then added. "I'm going back to Kansas City, back to university life, where things are safe, dull and boring and *safe.*"

He said nothing for a long time. Instead he stood on the veranda, water drops still in his hair from the shower, and stared off across the lake. Fishermen, some of the last of the season, sat in canoes outlined against the sky like boats in a painting. Eliot said nothing, and then he turned to look at her.

"You care what other people will think," he said. "People in restaurants. People on the street.

Your daughter. My mother. But what about what *you* think? What about what *I* think?" Maggie tried to respond in some way, with talk about how an individual's decision can affect so many lives, the way Joe's decision had. But wasn't she now thankful that her monotone world with Joe had come to an end, thankful that she'd been jolted into the sheer electricity of life, where events could hurt her again, but where events could also make her laugh, give her joy?

"I'm sorry," was all she could say. She wanted to tell him about Lucy, about how strongly she, Maggie, felt about motherhood. *A parent is there to set an example,* she'd say. *Lucy has been through one shock already, when she lost her father*. But she didn't say this because she knew what his response would be, *could* be. *You'll still be her parent, you'll always be there. This is your life we're talking about.*

"I'm disappointed in you," he finally said. "I thought you were stronger than that."

"Well, I guess I'm not," she answered. He nodded, looked again to the few canoes dotting the lake. By early summer, the lake would be crawling with speedboats, paddleboats, pontoon boats, boats, boats. Tourists. Tourists. Tourists. She had been so looking forward to a fresh summer in Little Bear Lake. A fresh start. Now, she felt she couldn't do it. Eliot had thought her strong. So had she. But apparently she was not.

"When are you leaving?" he asked, his voice barely above a whisper, but steady, angry almost.

"Today," she told him. "If I don't go now, I'm afraid I never will. I'm just packing a few things into the car. I'll ask Claire to pack the rest. She's on her way over here now." She told him this last fact knowing he would leave, knowing he wouldn't want Claire—wouldn't want anyone—to catch him in such a vulnerable moment. But if he didn't leave soon, Maggie was afraid that she might try to touch him one more time, touch the soft skin of his face, his hands. If she touched him, it would be her undoing. "I'm asking Claire to take over the Moon."

What had she thought he would say? What had she thought he would do? First he turned again to those few canoes, to the wide expanse of lake. He pointed toward the other end.

"I live there," he said, "in a house my father built. I grew up in that house. It'll probably be the house I'll be living in when it comes time for me to die." Maggie felt tears well up in her eyes, begin to cascade down her face. She hadn't wanted to cry, had promised herself she wouldn't, but she did. He reached down and grabbed her hand, pulled her up out of the rocker. He took her face firmly in his hands and turned her head toward the end of the lake. "Over there," he said again, forcing her to look, "is where I'll be if you change your mind. But don't take forever, Maggie. As the poet says, the bird of time is on the wing, remember?" He went down the steps to his truck and opened the door. Maggie watched as he rifled among papers in the glove compartment until he found an envelope. He brought it back to the veranda and held it out to her. Her hand shaky, she reached out and took it.

"I was going to give this to you last night, at the dance," Eliot said. "But I changed my mind. Read it sometime." And then he went back to his truck, where he stopped for a minute, his eyes still on the lake. He turned to look back at her, as if he was going to say something else, but if he was, he decided against it. He simply got into his truck, the engine roared to life, and once again Maggie saw him turn right at the stone fence, where the glorious swallows loved to build their summer nests. Then he was gone.

Claire was not so kind. She had skyrocketed into the driveway of the Moon, her little Chevy Vega riding on dust and air. Taking every other step, she had bounded up onto the huge veranda, her hair all aflutter without its customary bandanna, and found Maggie still sitting there in the rocker.

"I finally get an old friend back," Claire said, looking down at Maggie. "I finally get into a business in my old hometown, a thing I'd thought impossible. 'Claire, you're gonna die in Toronto and no one will even notice,' I used to tell myself. 'No business opportunities in your old hometown.' And then you come along and change all that, Maggie. And let's face it. You went for a pack of cigarettes twenty-five years ago, just left me sitting here. Then you turn up again, the prodigal friend, and I take you back. Now, you're leaving again. So tell me, Maggie. What are you running from this time? What's got you skittish this time around? A cog in the machine of life? I'll tell you something, my dear. Some of us deal with cogs daily. And now, here's another cog for me, and just hours after Mr. Right has finally shown up."

Maggie stood, the rocker still rocking beneath her, as though it seated a ghost. Robbie, maybe, sitting back in his customary way, smiling to hear Claire and Maggie squabbling over some incident in their lives. But Robbie wasn't there. He was dead.

"I obviously forgot that this was all about *Claire*," Maggie said. "How foolish of me." With this, Claire calmed down.

"I'll tell you what this is all about," she said. "It's about you and Eliot ending up in the sack and your guilt in handling it. For a month now we've all been tiptoeing around Robbie's memory, like it's something sacred. Well, I'm tired of it. You once broke his heart. Big deal. We all get our hearts broken at least once, Maggie. Some of us get them broken more than that. It's a part of life, especially when you're young. And here's another bulletin you may not like. Julia became the love of Robert Flaubert's life. So don't flatter yourself."

Maggie decided she had heard quite enough. She picked up her coffee cup. She would leave the dishes done when she left the little apartment, a habit she'd acquired from her mother. Her life might be in emotional shards, but the dishes, by God, *would be clean*.

"I'm taking just a few clothes," Maggie said. "I'll get Lakeview Movers to pack the rest of my things. You know very well that you can run this place by yourself. You can run this place in your sleep, which will be sporadic now that Mr. Right has truly arrived." She turned, on her way back to the screen door. Claire could stand on the porch and rant all she wanted. Maggie had some packing to do.

"And I'll tell you something else you might not know," Claire continued. "All of Little Bear Lake already suspects something between you and Eliot, just by watching you last night, Maggie. That's how it is in little towns, sweetie. Now, did anyone tar and feather you for it? No, they didn't. Everyone likes Eliot. And they seem to like you, too, and that's all that's important. Sure there will be some gossip. Younger man, older woman. Big deal. You didn't write the book on it, you know."

Now Maggie was angry. "Really?" She spun on her heel and faced Claire. "Well, what about you and Christopher Dean? What about your third husband? He was only twelve years younger and look what happened to *that* marriage!" Claire's eyes grew wide and round. At first Maggie thought she had truly offended her. But then Claire laughed, a deep rolling laugh.

"Christopher Dean?" she wanted to know. "You're comparing Eliot to *Christopher Dean?*" She clapped her hands together, obviously amused.

"He was a younger man," Maggie said, defending herself.

"Maggie, honey, Chris was the ultimate couch potato," Claire said. "Our life revolved around hockey games. That last year we were together, we only talked between periods. Emergencies were discussed during time-outs. You can't compare *Christopher Dean* to Eliot."

Maggie waved a hand, as if to dismiss Claire. "Eliot didn't go on like this," she said. And she realized for the first time that that had bothered her, hadn't it? He didn't say much at all. *I live in that house. The bird of time is on the wing.* He was wiser for this, Maggie knew, and something about it disturbed her.

"Eliot is hurt," said Claire. "I'm angry, and

that's the difference." Then she put her hand on Maggie's arm, and squeezed it.

"I'm just afraid, Claire," said Maggie. "And when you're afraid, you have to do what you think is best to protect yourself." Claire merely nodded.

Everyone does the best they can in the scheme of things. At least, that seemed like a reasonable notion. Maggie looked down at the envelope in her hand. In an instant she decided she would not read it that day. And perhaps not the next. Perhaps not until she was safely back in Kansas City, back waiting to begin another year of university classes. Maybe in the professor's lounge, while Mr. Walton was talking about his parrot, she would take the letter out of her purse and read the words then, in the heart of safety. Reading it now might change her mind.

"I just don't get it, Maggie," Claire said. "What *are* you running from?"

Maggie tried to answer her, tried to find a truth in it for herself, but she couldn't.

"I'm just taking a few things," she said. "I'll be ready in thirty minutes." She would have a car this time, no plane to carry her up over lakes and mountains and clouds and dreams that linger close to the earth. She would not rise like the Phoenix, or like Nixon in his helicopter, rising up over the smoldering mess of his political career. She would not follow the birds through the sky on their southward migration. She would be earthbound, driving her little green car through a night and day of tire against tar, of telephone poles and highway signs rushing past her like the days of her life. She would be earthbound.

Claire sat down on the steps of the Moon, a great sigh escaping her. Maggie reached down and touched a hand to her friend's shoulder.

"So he's Mr. Right?" she asked, and Claire nodded.

"You know what they say," said Claire, and reached up to squeeze Maggie's trembling hand. "The fiftieth time tells the story."

hegira: any journey made for the sake of safety or as an escape; flight . . .

—From Maggie's old college dictionary

Ancestors, Little Bear Cemetery

THE SECOND LEAVING

Because I could not stop for Death,
He kindly stopped for me;
. . . .
Since then 'tis centuries; but each
Feels shorter than the day
I first surmised the horses' heads
Were toward eternity.

—EMILY DICKINSON,
FROM MAGGIE'S COLLEGE TEXTBOOK

The cemetery at Little Bear Lake looked more like a rolling park, set in among the permanent green of fir and spruce, then laced with the red and gold leaves of autumn. In driving past it for the month she'd been in Little Bear Lake, Maggie had never once glanced toward the blanket of stones that covered the hillside. One of them was Robert Flaubert's, his last statement—that was why. He had been still alive in her memory of him, and finding his grave marker would be setting his spirit free at last, releasing the ghost. She hadn't been ready for that, not until now. Now she was on her way out of town, the letter from Eliot in her purse, her suitcase packed and in the trunk of her car, her heart feeling as though it might burst from the weight of the decision she was making: leaving Eliot, leaving Little Bear Lake. Stopping by the cemetery meant now or never. Maggie doubted she would ever be back this way again.

She found the stone in the most unexpected way. She had been walking through the older part of the cemetery, her heart racing, her blood beating in her ears. Along the side of the creek bank were the stones of ancestors, some Robert Flaubert's, most likely, and Eliot's. Ancestors who came to Little Bear Lake and lived their lives in the houses they built with pride. And then, after doing their best, or failing to do so, they died and went back to the earth. *I live there,* Eliot had said, *in a house my father built. And I'll probably be living there when the time comes for me to die.* The stones of the ancestors of Little Bear Lake, the first settlers and founders, dotted the bank of Little Bear Creek, a place cluttered nicely with birches and aspens and mountain ash, the latter of which were covered with brilliant red berries, berries to liven up the long white of the winter that was to come, and to feed the birds that would need them to survive.

Maggie passed through the older stones and

made her way toward the ones which appeared to be newer. Funny, but a person could die and be buried and the world would go right on turning. No matter how rich they were, how famous, how much they knew about tamarack trees and the eating habits of screech owls. The world spun on. After hearing the terrible news from Claire, Maggie had thought about that day of Robbie's funeral, wondered what small event had been taking place in her own life in Kansas City at the same time that Robbie went back to join the soil of his ancestors. Maudy told her it had been in spring, when the wild cherry had just burst into bloom along the ridges, and the warblers had returned from their winter in warmer climes. What had Maggie been doing in Kansas City? Grading papers? More important, what had she been doing the very second in time when Robert Flaubert had reached a hand up to grasp his heart, knowing that it was about to kill him? Life was a funny filmstrip, when you considered it for what it really was, a strip of celluloid recording some quite unremarkable circumstances: She might very well have been soaking in a bubble bath the instant Robert died. She might have been gardening, complaining about tennis elbow, upset that the pizza she had ordered was late. A Marx Brothers film, life.

This is what she thought as she passed through

the moss-covered older stones and made her way up a small hill. And then, as if on cue from some invisible stage director, there appeared the most brilliant orange butterfly, fluttering happily about Maggie's head. She tried to follow its wavering flight, in and out among the headstones, up and down. Robbie had taught her to identify many butterflies during those three summers, a knowledge which she had passed on to Lucy. He had left things behind, Robert had, in people he had never even met. It was a monarch, Maggie could tell as it lit upon a stone and stayed there, its burnt-orange wings traced with black veins and sprinkled with white spots along the margins. The monarch, the only butterfly to migrate annually, both north and south, as birds do. The fragile little monarch. And then it rose, straight up into the air like a tiny orange helicopter, and that's when Maggie saw the others, thousands of them forming a long orange ribbon in the sky: The monarchs were migrating! She had only read about them, only guessed what it must be like to see that steady stream of orange rising up to catch the winds, butterflies on their way to Mexico! *No single butterfly makes the entire journey,* Robbie had told her once, when they had happened upon a monarch feeding on some milkweed. *They winter in a valley in Mexico, ten thousand feet high. Over fourteen billion of them on just four acres. They turn the trees there orange*. And then the single butterfly joined the others. The wide orange ribbon waved and undulated. Maggie knew it would grow longer as it went, picking up more travelers. Then, as she stood among the stones in Little Bear Cemetery, the monarchs crested the horizon of treetops and were gone. Maggie had been stunned at the sight of them, felt honored to be given that rare glimpse. And that's when she looked down and saw that the stone in front of her, the stone on which the lonely monarch had lit, said ROBERT FLAUBERT, BORN DECEMBER 16, 1943, DIED MAY 2, 1990. HERE HE LIES WHERE HE LONGED TO BE, HOME IS THE SAILOR, HOME FROM THE SEA, AND THE HUNTER HOME FROM THE HILL. Robert's grave marker. Maggie felt her eyes grow watery, and yet, she felt rejuvenated in some strange way, revitalized. He had loved that poem, "Requiem," by Robert Louis Stevenson, and so she was not surprised to see that it had been chosen for his epitaph. Stevenson's own marker bore this poem as its inscription. And like Robbie, he, too, had been buried on a hilltop.

" 'Under the wide and starry sky,' " Maggie recited. She could still remember all the words to "Requiem" from high school. This would be her own eulogy to Robbie, finally, at last, a eulogy to a dear friend. " 'Dig the grave and let me lie. Glad did I live, and gladly die, And I laid me down with a will. This be the verse you grave for me: *Here he lies where he longed to be; Home is the sailor, home from the sea, And the hunter home from the hill.'* " She had broken a sprig of mountain ash berries as she passed along the bank near the creek, a bunch so dazzlingly red they could have been rubies. The birds could spare this single branch. Maggie leaned forward and placed the berries on Robert Flaubert's grave. HERE HE LIES WHERE HE LONGED TO BE. From across the cemetery voices rose up, getting closer and closer, family or friends coming to visit the memory of their loved ones. Maggie backed away from the stone, looking hard at it one more time. HOME IS THE SAILOR, HOME FROM THE SEA. Then she looked up into the sky where there was now no trace that a river of butterflies had ever rippled through that part of the heavens.

"Good-bye, Roberto," she said, remembering her silly little nickname for him, a nickname only because she had liked the sound of it upon her tongue. "Good-bye, Roberto."

Maggie pulled off the highway just before hitting the 401, which would carry her to Toronto, and then on to Horseshoe Falls, where she would cross the border to begin her journey west. She would be racing the monarch butterflies, migrating herself, looking for an altitude somewhere to settle down safely. Safety had always been the operative word, hadn't it? New England safety. Don't rock the boat. Even if the boat is sinking, don't, don't, don't rock the boat. She pulled off the highway to think: *Why Kansas City?* That's what she kept asking herself. Why Kansas City when Joe was the only one left there? The girls were gone. She herself had only moved to Kansas City because it was Joe's hometown, and he had had an offer from a family acquaintance to practice law there. So why was she heading back to Kansas City? To be with Bridgette in the delivery room? Why wasn't she going to Boston, where her own ancestors were churning up soil, making rich fertilizer? Surely she could get a teaching position in Boston.

"Because Kansas City is the only home I know anymore," Maggie said, as cars rushed past her. And yet, the house on Beauchemin Street was gone to new owners. The girls were gone. Joe was in a new life. Only the university remained intact, waiting. "The only home I know," Maggie said again, as an immense sadness overwhelmed her. Like the cars hurtling past on the highway, the questions were coming too fast, and there were too many. *What are you running from this time?* Claire had asked. *Did you remember how Jay Gatsby stood on the end of his dock?* Eliot wanted to know. *You mean you don't care?* Lucy wondered, when she told Maggie that Joe would once again be a father. *Aren't you coming back to teach?* Anita had called two days earlier to ask. *What are you running from this time? What are you running from this time? What are you running from?*

Maggie pulled back into traffic, but an hour past Toronto she stopped at a tiny motel and rented a room for herself. She couldn't drive any longer, not when her mind was on the past, and on the future, on everything but the highway in front of her. Instead she sat on the lumpy bed of her motel room and tried to answer Claire's question. Her first real marathon had been the run from her brother Dougie's death, straight into marriage to Joe McIntyre and away from Robert Flaubert. She had run from her mother's death into courses on Literary Criticism, the English Sonnet, the Medieval Latin Lyric, anything to still her mind, make it work elsewhere. Running. So what was she so afraid of now? Dougie's death was no longer a likely answer. Her mother had been gone for over ten years. What now? Claire was right. She was running, no doubt about it. What had been her favorite Yeats poem? The one about the glimmering girl: *It had become a glimmering girl, With apple blossom in her hair, Who called me by my name and ran, And faded through the brightening air.* This had been the poem she had remembered that day in the attic, just a few months earlier, the day she went through the dusty boxes and found the cologne-drenched handkerchief from Robert Flaubert. Poems, like butterflies, migrate. Yeats had followed her to Canada. And what about the poem's ending? *Though I am old with wandering, Through hollow lands and hilly lands, I will find out where she has gone, And kiss her lips, and take her hands; And walk among long dappled grass, And pluck till time and times are done, The silver apples of the moon, The golden apples of the sun*. This whole crazy journey of hers, this hegira, had been because of Yeats, because of that old paper of his that she had gone into her attic on Beauchemin Street to find, for Jennifer Fulbright. It had all started with Yeats. She had loved him more dearly than any of the other poets, and had eventually moved T. S. Eliot into second place. Eliot Flaubert had no idea how close he had come to being named "Yeats." But Maggie had grown to love Yeats more because she knew all about those "apples of time," didn't she? Especially the silver ones. How many times had she wakened in the heart of a Kansas City night, Joe snoring beside her, and remembered Robbie Flaubert in his silver canoe, on his silver lake, with his silver skin, in her silver memory of him? *The silver apples of the moon*. Was Claire right? Was Maggie just caught up with the romance of the past? Is that what Robert Flaubert had been representing to her all these years? *Don't flatter yourself,* Claire had said. *Julia became the love of his life*. A lot of silver apples had come and gone, golden apples, and now someone else was calling Maggie by her name. Eliot. Would she let him, too, fade through the brightening air? *Mr. Einstein says the past exists,* Robbie had said. *We just can't see it*. Did it exist in Eliot? Was it okay to embrace feelings you had as a younger person? Who says exhilaration should disappear with age? Maggie had felt like a college girl again, in Eliot's arms. Was that so wrong?

The room she rented for the night was small and cramped, but clean. It reminded her of the very room she had rented in Little Bear Lake the night she learned that Robbie had died, and she had read his letters all night long, until dawn discovered her still alive, still able to face her future. *Dear Mags. There's a light wind tonight on Little Bear. And just a sliver of moon over the cove. It's lonely in autumn, with everyone and everything gone, the leaves, even the geese. Sometimes, I feel like we've been left behind here, the way tourists leave behind things they no longer want.* Was this what Eliot was feeling now?

After a hot bath, Maggie got into bed in her

motel room, as though she were getting inside a protective skin, and tried to sleep. She would drive west tomorrow, along the southern border of Lake Erie, through Cleveland, and on to Chicago. At Chicago she would turn south, taking Interstate 65, and somewhere near there she would spend another night. Then she would rise and wash and dress and set her sights on St. Louis. From there, she would turn to the west and drive toward the sun, which should be setting just as she pulled into Kansas City. Maybe Anita would meet her for dinner at that new Thai restaurant on Danner Boulevard. It was Maggie's turn to buy.

In the morning she called Anita, who was all bubbly energy and excited to hear Maggie's voice.

"Did I catch you at a bad time?" Maggie asked.

"Yes, you did," Anita answered. "I'm doing dishes, so thank you so much for calling to rescue me. When are you coming home? Now listen to this latest scoop, Maggie, honey. You have got to meet the new head of the English Department. He's tall compared to, well, he's tall at least as department heads go, maybe five foot eight. He wears these little heels on his shoes, so it's hard to tell. And he has brown eyes and hair peppered with gray, thinning hair, but the gray makes him what is generally known as *dignified*."

"Anita, you've never been especially good at playing Cupid," Maggie told her. "Remember how you set Marcie Blankenship up with Tony Simpson and they almost killed each other at the restaurant on their first date?" She could hear Anita rattling pans at the other end of the phone line. She imagined her there, in her kitchen in Kansas City, just seven blocks from Beauchemin Street, her hands in dishwater, the late fall sun beating into the room, catching the auburn highlights in her hair. Anita had been a good friend.

"Who says a food fight isn't a good way to start a relationship?" Anita was asking, her voice playful.

"I believe they threw more than food," Maggie said. "Weren't *knives* involved?" Anita ignored this. The clanking, metallic sound of pans being stacked now filtered over the phone wires.

"Anyway," Anita continued, "Henry is divorced. Thankfully, the ex-wife lives in another state. Well, actually, she lives across the state line in Kansas, but she only comes to Kansas City on weekends. I've told Henry all about you, Maggie, and, like Barkus, he's willing. And you know, I honestly think that if he were away from the English Department for a few days, or a few weeks, he would have a terrific sense of humor."

Maggie smiled. "Let's see if I've got this straight, Anita," she said. "You want to set me up with a short, humorless, balding man who spends weekends with his ex-wife and wears shoe lifts." There was a long pause on the other end of the phone.

"I didn't say he was Robert Redford," said Anita. "Call me when you get here."

Maggie hung up the phone and ordered coffee from a take-out café next door to the motel. Then she seat-belted herself into the car and began her latest hegira by pulling slowly into the stream of cars that was shooting past on Highway 401. Her little car was green as summer, unlike the wild red of the leaves on the rock maple back at Little Bear Lake. She merged easily into traffic, as though it were now the flow of her life, her brake lights flicking on now and then until the cars of strangers swallowed her up. She was disappearing. Lost to her own life's decisions. As she drove, she thought about Eliot. What would he do? What would become of him? Would life treat him as well as he deserved? She thought about Eliot, while behind her Little Bear Lake fell backward, as if into a blue dream. She imagined that the loons would cry their cry just as the sun set upon the waters. She tried to picture it in her mind. At least for a while, Eliot would be standing on a dock near the Harvest Moon, looking out across the water for a shimmering light that would not, *could not*, shine. He would do this until another one of life's tentacles reached out and pulled him away, reeled him into the bosom of another dream that he would live, with a young woman who would bear their children, who would be there for him in the heart of those lonely nights that were sure to come. They come for everyone, once in a while. And Eliot would learn to treasure the path of his life, with his wife and children, and he would regret the day in his great old age that he would have to leave it. But behind him would be his own children, the results of those choices he made in life. And here, Maggie knew, is where the dream would carry itself forward, up on those wings that can rise above the fragile green lights that shimmer across the blue waters, the kind of light Jay Gatsby knew well. Eliot would *survive.*

Just before Maggie crossed the border, she pulled into a picnic area on the Canadian side and sat staring at the trees of autumn, which unfolded all around her. The truth was that it didn't feel right, this trip back. It didn't feel the way it did when she was driving toward Little Bear Lake. The last time she had driven away, in 1969, she did not know that she would never see Robert Flaubert again. She had driven toward her brother's death, and then her marriage and her two daughters, and her mother's death, and her Ph.D. If she drove away this time, she would probably never be back. She had been trying hard not to think of losing Eliot. Trying hard not to remember the words she had spoken just the night before, in her little motel room, when she woke sweaty and nightmarish, her pajamas soaked, to whisper, "I love you, Eliot. I love you." She should have told him that, should have told him the truth.

As cars zoomed past her, the drivers all seemingly certain of their futures, anxious to get them over with, Maggie suddenly remembered something Joe had told her, the day he stood in their little parlor, just a year earlier. He was explaining why he couldn't stay in the marriage any longer. To Maggie it had been just rhetoric, coming at her as she sat with her glass of sherry and stared at the first editions in her bookcase. But now she remembered the words, and they seemed to mean something more; now they seemed custom-ordered. "I feel like I'm being swept along by this," Joe had told her. "It's like riding in a fast-moving car with no reverse. All I can do is try to steer as best I can. And I know I can't take any U-turns, Maggie. I know that once I go, I can't come back. This is a long stretch of straight road, but I'm willing to suffer all consequences." And so he was. Well, good for Joe McIntyre. Maggie reached into her purse and pulled out the envelope Eliot had given her the day before. With cars whizzing past, the wind from their wake gently rocking her own car, she opened the envelope. She had expected a letter from Eliot inside, but to her surprise that's not what she found. The letter was dated October 3, 1969. *Dear Rob,* it began. *Last week, somewhere in the Mekong Delta, my brother Dougie was killed. He died in a war we should not be fighting, a war he wanted no part of. But Dougie is dead, and already my own life is changed. Already, I can no longer look upon the world as I once did. I wish I could tell you this in person, so you will better understand. Some lives are shorter than others, but while we live the ones we got, we need to live them fully. This is something Dougie was denied, but this is his legacy to me. We've shared three wonderful summers together, but I'm too young to settle down with one notion of life right now. Maybe, some day in the future, you and I will meet again. Until then, I hope that you will think of me fondly, as I will you. I now believe that love is like absolute zero. It's only possible in theory. But I hope that you find love, Rob. And if the day ever comes that I find it, too, I'll grab hold of it, the way Dougie would want me to. Life is too short and precious to do it any other way. And, as you yourself know, the bird of time is on the wing. Take care of yourself. Love, Maggie.*

For minutes that were long as hours Maggie sat

in the gently rocking car, on the edge of the highway, the letter in her hand. How could time have been such a trickster? How could she have remembered, for all those years, that she had left Robert Flaubert *after* she met Joe? How had guilt gotten mixed in with the facts? How had she recalled a short, abrupt note: *Good-bye. So long. Hasta la vista, pal, it's been swell.* She had already left the notion of a future with Robbie behind, before she even met Joe McIntyre! But somewhere in there among the diapers, and school papers, and flat tires, and basketball games, and visits to the dentist, the facts of her first romance had grown larger. Up in the heat and dust and dark of her attic, where she had hidden Robbie's letters, the truth had grown and expanded, like a large mushroom spreading out over the years. Her episode in time with Robert Flaubert had been a case of First Love and nothing more. Claire was right. But then, Claire was an impartial observer. Claire would know. But worse yet, how could Maggie have forgotten the truths she learned from Doug's death: *We need to live life fully. If the day ever comes that I find love, I'll grab hold of it, the way Dougie would want me to. Absolute zero. Bird of time*. Truths that Eliot had quoted back to her.

Maggie looked out at the straight piece of road

that lay before her, a road that would carry her on to Niagara Falls, and back to the heartland of America. She eased the car into gear and then pulled back onto the highway.

"Once I go," Maggie said aloud, "I can't come back."

Canada Geese Returning

THE JOURNEY HOME: THE EPILOGUE

home ***(OE* ham, *dwelling):*** the place in which one's domestic affections are centered . . .

—FROM MAGGIE'S OLD COLLEGE DICTIONARY

epilogue: a speech delivered by one of the actors at the end of a play . . .

—FROM MAGGIE'S OLD COLLEGE DICTIONARY

We carry in our bones part of our ancestors' marrow, and on those bones we are clothed in skin, the cells of which partly belong to them. Sometimes, whether rightly or wrongly, we carry our ancestors' inhibitions, their failures, their aspirations, their successes. Something of her old New England upbringing had gotten hold of Maggie Patterson, gotten hold and tried to suffocate her. At least, that's how it felt to her now. But this time, she wouldn't let it. This time, she would rise above it. She would rise up, like that old Greek phoenix, out of the ashes of a marriage burned away. She would take to the sky like the monarchs, on the wings of her new life, daring to fly so far, daring to try it.

The drive back to Little Bear Lake took five hours. As the white line kept disappearing beneath her car, Maggie felt as if she were being reeled back. She had already phoned Claire.

"Don't write 'Director' on your chair yet," Maggie told her. "Your partner is on her way home."

"Does this mean I'm going to have to listen to 'Some Enchanted Evening' for the rest of my life?" Claire asked. "By the way, just who the hell *is* Ezio Pinza?"

If the past exists, then it cannot be changed. Only the future is flexible. Only the future is something to be taken on, challenged, made as perfect or imperfect as lowly human beings dream it to be. *Love is like absolute zero,* Eliot had quoted her. *It's only possible in theory*. Well, maybe Maggie had said that once, but she no longer believed it. *Scientists have recorded temperatures one millionth of a degree above absolute zero,* she would tell Eliot again. *Close isn't just good in horseshoes. It's good in love, too.*

It was early afternoon when she saw the WELCOME TO LITTLE BEAR LAKE sign, and she felt a truth in it. She felt *welcome* there. She passed the cemetery first, then the big hanging sign, THE HARVEST MOON, DANCING & COCKTAILS. But she didn't turn in at the stone fence. She kept going until she reached the place where the birches clustered together, protecting the moss beneath them, and where the small sturdy dock pushed out into the lake. There was no sign of Eliot. She felt a wave of terror rise up. What if he was gone? What if he no longer wanted her? Could the bird of time have flown already, flown so quickly?

The road around the lake was red and yellow and orange. Autumn had come rapidly, like a spreading fire. It seemed as if overnight the scenery had gone from *hinting*—what with those swatches of superb color along the hills—to being *overwhelmed*. Autumn had truly arrived in Little Bear Lake. There was now a hurriedness in how the squirrels scampered about, gathering hazelnuts, in how the birds scurried in the treetops and along the ground. *Winter,* that's what the hurriedness said. *Winter is coming!* Maggie would need to have a load of hardwood delivered and split and stacked for the winter, fuel to keep the big fireplace fed at the Moon. She remembered its snapping and popping from years earlier, during those harvest moon dances when the weather had turned cold. Now, it would sing to her all winter. And she would need to take Eliot's advice and have the big dance room winterized, the old windows replaced with modern ones designed to keep the cold at bay.

She saw his truck first, driven close to the front steps of the house that Robert Flaubert had built and then set about raising a family in. It was a sturdy house, with natural wood so that it would blend in with nature, brown as bark, sitting in the heart of a tract of birches. A huge deck circled three fourths of it, a perfect place to watch trout jumping in the lake, and migrating hawks, and setting suns, and full moons filling up the night sky like shiny half-dollars. Maggie got out of her car and gently closed the door. Behind her, somewhere on the autumn ridge that ran like a spine, like a colored backbone around Little Bear Lake, she heard the cry of the northern raven, a faint echo in the distance. She followed the path that led around the house, her feet seeming to know something about it already, a path that led down to the lake. Eliot was standing down there, by the edge of the water, looking out across it, at the Moon maybe. He was standing there, shoulders straight, the warm autumn sun drenching him, burnishing him, turning him golden. The way the moon had turned Robert Flaubert silver.

"Eliot," Maggie said, and as soon as she released the word from her mouth, she knew that she was home. The word was lifted up, set free from the earth, lifted above those crimes, misfortunes and follies of mankind. And Maggie, too, was freed, free to live, free to love, free to settle down in a lovely town by a lovely lake, her own niche in time. *Close isn't just good in horseshoes.*

"Eliot," she said more loudly. This time, he heard her. And then he was turning toward her, not in silver, not in the magic of moonlight, where things can appear more wonderful than they are, but with the autumn sun setting his hair afire with amber light, he was turning toward her, the orbit of his life spinning into hers. *The hunter home from the hill.* And then she was running, the white birches blurring, the lake itself rising up to meet her.

Don't miss the latest novel
by K. C. McKinnon!

CANDLES ON BAY STREET

Published in hardcover by
Doubleday Books.
Available in bookstores everywhere.

Please read on
for an exciting excerpt from this
wonderful new novel . . .

ONE

"Every time you light a candle, an angel is born."
—DEE DEE MICHAUD, SPRING 1997

She was the childhood sweetheart I wanted to marry, but didn't. I blame General Motors for this. In 1982, when their new line of sleek Corvettes came off the assembly line, Bobby Langford bought one, a shiny gold, the color of the sun. And he looked so good sitting behind the wheel that Dee Dee Michaud fell head over heels in love with *him*, instead of me. There I was, standing at the curb and about to make my big move. The rest, as Neanderthal man might say, is prehistory.

I don't remember not knowing who she was. Hers is the very first face I can pull up when I flip back through the flimsy pages of my memory. She was part of my history, my family folklore, my roots: At times, it seemed as if she were a part of *me*. We were both two years old when she moved in next door, accompanied by Estelle and Marvin Michaud, who were known around our little town of Fort Kent, Maine, as "older parents." They had just bought the two-story Victorian next door to us at 204 Bay Street. I'm told that we met for the first time, officially, at my third birthday party a few weeks later. I can't remember this, but I have the pictures as proof. Even then she was ravishing, a two-and-a-half-year-old flirt, her party hat canted to one side of her head, wheat-colored curls exploding from beneath the rim. And in her eyes a bright mischievous fire that I thought would never go out. When we were five years old we took a bath together, in a big galvanized tub in the backyard. That's a hot photo I've been carrying in my wallet since the seventh grade, when I slipped it out of my mom's scrapbook, unbeknownst to anyone but me. Ross Cloutier was the only person who knew about the picture. "What would you say if I told you that I have in my wallet a picture of Dee Dee Michaud naked as a jaybird?" I asked. We were sitting at the edge of the potato field, on the outskirts of town, smoking Salem cigarettes and getting sick to our stomachs. "I'd tell you pigs could fly," Ross answered. I didn't bother to prove him wrong. I told myself it was because I was defending Dee Dee's honor. But the real reason I didn't show him the picture is that I'm sitting in the galvanized tub, crying my eyes out with embarrassment, while Dee Dee is dancing like a dervish, silver drops of water cascading down her back.

This has been the story of our lives.

When we were in the third grade Dee Dee beat up Vincent Cyr for beating *me* up. She was taller than me in those days. I hadn't yet started "sprouting up," as my mother predicted I would, an act that sounded terrifying to me. I would lie in bed at night and imagine myself looking like a large, radiation-ridden potato after the "sprouting" was over. But it seemed I had no stomach for Salems *or* fighting, in those days before the sprouting could occur. So Dee Dee fought my battles for me. When she returned the comic book Vinny had taken from me, I should've been embarrassed that a girl had come to my rescue. But I wasn't. "Here, Sammy," she said. "I think you dropped something." I looked up into those blue-gray eyes, deeper and bluer than the old swimming hole in the St. John River, and they were so sincere that I really *believed* I'd dropped the comic book after all. That was her power. That was Dee Dee.

In the fifth-grade talent show we were Bogey and Bacall in *Key Largo*. We fought about it for almost a month, right up to the night of the performance: Dee Dee wanted to be Bogey. It was the only time I never gave in to her.

Our freshman year of high school she was expelled for a week, for using profanity and smoking cigarettes in the bathroom. Her mother asked me to talk to her, so I did. "Your mother says you're running with some very wild girls," I said to Dee Dee. "Would you please introduce me to them?"

We formed a band our sophomore year, called the Acute Angles, because all four of us had geometry together. Dee Dee sang, I played lead guitar, Ross Cloutier played bass, and Brian LeBlanc played drums. We even managed to get a few gigs in town, but then Brian moved away and we couldn't find the heart to go on without him. Yet my greatest concern in those days was finding a way to get Dee Dee to stop the "buddy" thing and get straight to the sex. Otherwise, I feared I might die. On my tombstone would be the words: *Here lies the only male virgin in the Class of '82.*

A month before we graduated from high school Dee Dee started dating Bobby Langford. His parents were divorced and living in Connecticut, so they'd sent him north to the wilds, to live with his grandparents, thinking it would be good for Bobby. It was disaster for *me*. On the morning of our graduation, Dee Dee jumped into the passenger seat of my truck—a 1954 Ford pickup, an inheritance from my Grandpa Thibodeau that had taken me months to restore. On the drive to school, I decided to make my move. I would do it with humor—humor was what Dee Dee loved best. I'd be Woody Allen. I'd tell her, "Listen, I know we've been friends. Hell, we've been Bogey and Bacall. But maybe it's time we were something more. I tell you what. This time, I'll let you be Bogey." But before I could say anything Dee Dee showed me her engagement ring. "It's a secret," she said. "Nobody knows, so don't tell. Okay, Sammy?" I didn't wonder where Bobby got the money for a diamond ring *or* the Corvette. He was making trips to Connecticut twice a month and a lot of good pot was suddenly going around the streets of Fort Kent, Maine. I looked at the ring. "O Great God Cannabis, thank you for your rewards," I said. I thought it would make her laugh, but it didn't. "Don't believe rumors, Sammy," was all she said. "Talk is cheap in small towns."

The very next day after our high school graduation—and much to the disappointment of her parents and everyone who loved her—Dee Dee packed her suitcase. Then she and Bobby and the sun-colored Corvette sneaked out of Fort Kent during the night. I heard from her two weeks later, when I received a picture postcard of a huge ball of string sitting above the words: *Visit Jennings, Louisiana, Home of the World's Biggest Ball of Twine*. On the back she'd scribbled these words: *Dear Samuel Louis Thibodeau. Ain't life a hoot? Love, Dee Dee.*

The next we heard she and Bobby Langford

had gotten married. Mrs. Estelle Michaud, Dee Dee's mother, crossed the hedge that separated the Michauds' yard from ours and came sadly up the steps and into our kitchen to tell my mom the heartbreaking news. She didn't even bother to stop, as she usually did, to pick up any candy wrappers that might have blown into the yard, or empty pop cans that might have rolled in off the street. She didn't bother to pinch the dead leaves from around the flowers she'd planted in narrow beds along the hedge. Instead, she came directly into my mother's kitchen, the screen door slamming behind her like a bang of reality. "That crazy girl has finally done it, Margaret," I heard her tell my mother. "That crazy girl has gone and ruined her life." I was sitting with one leg up over the side of Dad's easy chair, counting the seconds until my first semester at college would begin and my life could be saved from the most complete and utter boredom ever wished upon an earthling—now that Dee Dee was gone from next door—but this got my full attention. This turned life interesting again, for I knew right away who *that crazy girl* was. I came to stand in the doorway, leaning in just enough to catch Mrs. Michaud's words, and that's how I learned that the love of my life, Diana Catherine Michaud, voted Biggest Class Flirt and Prettiest Girl for four years straight, had married the man behind the wheel of that golden chariot of a Corvette. "She's just a baby," Mrs. Michaud said, wringing her hands and looking generally miserable. A week later I got a second postcard, this time from Mankins, Texas. On the front was a picture of an enormous shoe: *Home of the World's Largest Cowboy Boot,* the heading read. On the back she'd written: *Dear Sammy, I'm so glad to be out of school and finally learning things about the world. Love, Dee Dee.* I pinned the postcard to the wall over the desk in my bedroom, next to the first one she'd sent, the ball-of-twine wonder. Then I took out the acceptance letter I'd received earlier that year from the University of Maine at Fort Kent, the small college in my hometown, and I reread all the words carefully. Some folks love to travel, it's true, but I knew then, a short time after graduating as valedictorian of Fort Kent High School's Class of 1982, that I would stay in my own town to finish college, aiming for a degree in science and biology. Then I would go off to vet school in Boston—as close to home as possible—for the four years it would take to complete a doctorate of veterinary medicine. But I would come home to my roots, and open a small animal practice in Fort Kent, where there was none. Like a lot of New England males I've known in my life, I'm the kind of man who stays close to hearth and kin. There's something in this northern Maine soil that has held me firmly to it. I should have known back then what this meant:

A crazy girl who is wild as the wind wants a boy who is just as wild. Yet the unfairness of it all overwhelmed me. I couldn't compete with Bobby Langford by driving around in Grandpa Thibodeau's truck. A 1954 pickup against a new Corvette? What woman besides Grammie Thibodeau would turn down the 'vette? Bobby Langford wasn't much at all without that car, but cars have a lot of power. Let's face it. Who would remember James Dean if he had died in a rusting, dented Volkswagen Rabbit? That silver Spider Porsche did it. My eyes filling with warm tears I never wanted anyone to see, I looked up at the two postcards again: *Ain't life a hoot?* Dee Dee had asked me. I tried to imagine her sitting atop the world's biggest ball of twine, or lying flat out on the toe of the largest cowboy boot, but the images wouldn't come. My only regret in life up to that short point of eighteen years had been that Dee Dee Michaud never slowed down long enough for me to *tell her* that she was the love of my life. I looked back down at the acceptance letter, and the catalogue newly arrived from Boston's School of Veterinary Medicine. I touched the tip of my index finger to each one. "There's the rest of your life, Sammy Thibodeau," I said aloud. "Get used to it." How could I have known then about life's tricks, about those smoky mirrors and false doors, one of which would bring Dee Dee Michaud home to Fort Kent and back into my life again? I couldn't. Just as Dee Dee couldn't know that her shaky marriage to Bobby Langford wouldn't last. In 1987, one year after I would graduate *summa cum laude* from the University of Maine at Fort Kent, word went around town that Dee Dee opened some kind of crafts shop in Wyoming—which sounded like the *other* end of the universe from northern Maine. The world spun on.

In February of the following year, Dee Dee's father died of a heart attack. I didn't come home from Boston for his funeral. I had an exam that week and vet school was tough. But Mother phoned to say that Dee Dee hadn't changed much. Now that Mr. Michaud was gone, Mrs. Michaud was making plans to move in with her widowed sister. She would rent out the house at 204 Bay Street. Mother would miss her old neighbor of so many years. So would I. Somehow, the notion of Dee Dee's folks still next door to mine had kept the memory alive for me. Before she hung up my mother said, "Oh, Sammy, I almost forgot. Dee Dee's eight months pregnant."

A month later, in March of 1988, two full years before I moved back to Fort Kent and opened my own practice, Mother wrote that Dee Dee Michaud had had her baby, a son she named

Martin. No one seemed to know if Bobby Langford was passing out cigars. The news of the birth was followed months later by news that Bobby had gotten a good job working on the Alaskan pipeline. I imagined that he and his gold Corvette had headed north together, toward the Land of the Midnight Sun. After that, no one seemed to know anything about Dee Dee Michaud anymore. Months passed, and I woke up one day to realize that I'd heard nothing from her, or *about* her. The ties that bind seem to have been finally severed. I imagined that the gossips were busy back in our hometown, digging for details of her life. But I was busy, too. I had my final and hardest year of vet school yet to live through. And, oh yes, I had asked a vet student named Lydia Newhart to marry me.

Ain't life a hoot?

To this day I have never bought an automobile from General Motors. It's just a matter of principle.

At my clinic, long after everyone has gone home, I still allow myself to think about Dee Dee. First loves die hard. If it's almost twilight, her memory comes more easily: that late afternoon in the summer of 1976, when we were both twelve, the summer we learned all the words to "Fernando." It was our favorite song that whole year long, a hit by the Swedish group ABBA. Lying on our stomachs that summery day, searching for crayfish in the murky water under rocks, Dee Dee turned to me and said, "I want to be ABBA when I grow up, Sammy." I scoffed. "You can't be a whole band, idiot," I told her. I was just beginning to realize that I would love her all my life, and that's why I had begun to call her *idiot*, and *monkey*, and *nitwit*. She was changing, too. The tomboy in her could turn soft and girlish with just a quick flash of expression. The tomboy in her was surfacing less and less. And there I was, locked in my skinny body which had started to grow tall without filling out, a body that would soon be pumping enough testosterone to fill the rock quarry out on Morin Road. Just then Dee Dee started to sing, a song about freedom fighters crossing the Rio Grande by starlight, the air around them alive and brimming with passion, fighting for liberty at any cost. Dee Dee, singing "Fernando" for the millionth time. Suddenly, she turned, skipped a rock out across the water. "I want to be a revolutionary, Sammy," she said. "I want to be like those people in the song, fighting for liberty under the stars." She stopped talking and looked over at me. "Kiss me, Sammy," she said. "With your tongue and everything. I wanna know what it feels like." Looking back, I know now that what I felt first that day was sadness. We were being taken away, purloined by time, our bodies changing without our permission. I could feel the day lurking just at our heels when our innocence would be wrested away forever. Why couldn't we stay right where we were, with our moms putting cold glasses of milk and warm cookies on the kitchen counter for us to find? With our sexuality still buried deep enough that it wouldn't hurt us?

"Listen," I said to her. "You been following me around too much lately and it's starting to get on my nerves." I said it to hurt her, only sensing in my growing bones that the day would come when I'd lie in my bed at night, aching for just the sight of her, knowing that she was on her front porch, right next door at 204 Bay Street, with Bobby "Octupus Hands" Langford hanging on to her as if she might evaporate. "You're never gonna be anything, anyway," I told her. "You're a nitwit." And then I climbed to the top of the little hill to get away from her. Funny how that day stays fresh in my memory: I replay it over and over again. Sometimes, I'm sitting in the office at my clinic, looking down at some lab report, when her twelve-year-old face suddenly materializes in my mind's eye. Or I'm cleaning dead leaves out of the downspouts when I hear her words, coming back at me. Maybe she, too, sensed what was happening, that our safe world was changing. Or maybe she knew that my anger at her wasn't real, that it was the only language I was equipped with then. After all, I was only a gangly boy whose body was jutting toward manhood. She had simply flopped over on her back and stared up at me, her blue-gray eyes the color of that northern Maine sky, her thick hair that had already turned from towhead to brownish blond splaying out about a face that would evolve into that of a beautiful woman.

"Hey, Fernando!" Dee Dee shouted up to me. "Can you hear the guns, baby?"

To this day I have a huge poster of ABBA hanging on the wall, behind my office door. It keeps me focused on the important things in life.